"Will you have dinner w

She tipped her head to the

"I guess so."

"You guess so?"

"You said it yourself. I'm used to classy." She didn't want to make this too easy for him. With that pretty face and muscled body, she doubted he ever had to work hard to get a date.

"Oh, I'll give you classy, Ferrin," he said. "You just wait and see. I'll be back at six."

"I'll be ready at six thirty," she said.

He threw his head back and laughed. "You're a minx."

Doubtful. But she was tired of the same-old, same-old, and Hunter promised something different.

"Six thirty, then."

She led him down the hall and opened the front door, leaning back as he brushed past her. But he stopped and put his hand on her chin.

Dinner suddenly seemed like more than just a break in the routine. She suspected he might want something from her but that was okay. She wanted something from him too. A chance to remember she was young and single. Maybe make a memory in California that wasn't laced with guilt and disappointment.

* * *

His Seduction Game Plan is part of the Sons of Privilege series by *USA TODAY* bestselling author Katherine Garbera

Dear Reader,

I'm so excited about this book. I hope you enjoyed King's story in *His Baby Agenda*. King and Hunter were spawned from my love of news media and hours of reading online about college kids and the mistakes they sometimes make. Also my love of football. When I was growing up, Sundays were for the NFL, and my dad—who had no sons, only three daughters—watched the games with us.

He taught us the rules of the game and we cheered for our perrenial favorites, the Miami Dolphins. My parents had met and married in south Florida, and going to the Dolphin games was a tradition with them.

Hunter grew up in this kind of family, but in Texas. He has brothers and he loves the game. Ferrin not so much. She's like me: she can't catch anything thrown at her. And, unlike my dad, her father didn't see that having a kid to pass on your passions to was enough. He really wanted a boy, and Ferrin knew she'd never measure up to his surrogate sons—his football players.

Ferrin and Hunter are both a little bit broken, something I think we all are at our core, and need each other and love to fix them. It's not that they have to change for each other, it's more that they both fill in the gaps of what's missing in the other.

This story was one of my favorites to write, probably because I was thinking about all those Sundays watching the Dolphins with my dad.

Happy reading!

Katherine Garbera

KATHERINE GARBERA

HIS SEDUCTION GAME PLAN

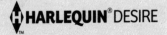
HARLEQUIN® DESIRE

Recycling programs
for this product may
not exist in your area

ISBN-13: 978-0-373-73461-0

His Seduction Game Plan

Copyright © 2016 by Katherine Garbera

Printed in U.S.A.

USA TODAY bestselling author **Katherine Garbera** is a two-time MAGGIE® Award winner who has written more than seventy books. A Florida native who grew up to travel the globe, Katherine now makes her home in the Midlands of the UK with her husband, two children and a very spoiled miniature dachshund. Visit Katherine on the web at katherinegarbera.com, or catch up with her on Facebook and Twitter.

Books by Katherine Garbera

HARLEQUIN DESIRE

Miami Nights

Taming the VIP Playboy
Seducing His Opposition
Reunited...With Child

Baby Business

His Instant Heir
Bound by a Child
For Her Son's Sake

Sons of Privilege

The Greek Tycoon's Secret Heir
The Wealthy Frenchman's Proposition
The Spanish Aristocrat's Woman
His Baby Agenda
His Seduction Game Plan

Visit her Author Profile page at Harlequin.com, or katherinegarbera.com, for more titles.

I know I mention them often in my dedication, but this one is for my parents, David and Charlotte Smith, who raised me to believe I could do anything. They have always been incredibly supportive of my writing even though no one in our family had ever done anything in the creative arts and they had no idea if I could earn a living from it. I wouldn't have been able to write if they hadn't been there for me. I love you both very much.

Special thanks to my agent Amanda Leuck for always having my back.

One

"Hello, sunshine."

Ferrin Gainer forced a smile at the man who most days barely recognized her. She'd never been close to her father. He'd lived for football and for the trophies he displayed proudly in their formal living room. Having a daughter had been a huge disappointment to him. Having one who flinched every time a football came flying through the air at her had been an embarrassment.

She'd barely seen him after her parents divorced when she was ten. She was vaguely aware that two of his players—his honorary sons—had been accused of murder some ten years ago when she'd been fifteen. But even that hadn't made him want to bond with her. In fact, it had only been two heart attacks and a severe stroke that had made him reach out to her.

She was twenty-five and had hoped she'd be past the need for a bond with her father, but let's face it, she wasn't. She knew not all of her friends had good relationships with their families, but that was what she wanted for herself.

She and her mom were close. They talked to each other every day. Her mom hadn't been a huge fan of Ferrin taking a sabbatical from her teaching job at the University of Texas and coming to California to take care of her father, but had understood it.

As a professor of psychology, Ferrin had put herself under the microscope a few times and what she saw... well, it made her mad. She should be able to move on but somehow she couldn't. She didn't want to accept the fact that this relationship was horribly broken.

She would fix it.

Dammit.

"Hey, Coach. How are ya feeling today?" she asked. When she was little she'd tried calling him Dad a time or two but he always insisted she call him Coach. Even before her parents divorced.

"I'm okay," he said, slurring his words. The last stroke had seemed to sap his will. There was something inside him that seemed to be keeping him from recovering. She wondered if not being able to work out and stay physically fit for the first time in his life was affecting him.

She had no idea. He barely talked to her. She was tempted to leave him in the care of the two in-home nurses, but she didn't want to be that kind of daughter.

And she felt guilty.

She knew if her mom were in the bed, well, Ferrin would be here no matter what. She owed at least as much to the man who'd given her half her DNA.

"That's good to hear. It's a beautiful day today so after breakfast, we're going out to sit in the garden."

"No."

She ignored him and went to the windows to open the drapes. Coach liked to keep the room dark; she'd thought at first maybe he had some light sensitivity from the stroke but his doctors informed her he didn't. The only thing keeping him in the dark was his desire to hide. It was as if there was something emotional inside that was causing him to retreat from the world.

She opened up one heavy drape and then the others. The Pacific Ocean was visible from Coach's bedroom. The frothy surf contrasting with the deep blue water and the rolling waves promised relaxation. Something that had evaded her since the moment she'd arrived on the West Coast.

"Leave them," he said again, slurring his words.

She hated hearing him like that. As estranged as their relationship had always been, she'd liked that her dad was strong. And he wasn't anymore.

"Just while you eat your breakfast. Joy is bringing it up and I'm going to eat with you. You know I don't like eating in the dark."

Ferrin had found if she ate with her father then he finished most of his food. She suspected he ate so he didn't have to talk to her, and she didn't mind. The doctors said eating well and getting him out of the bed were the keys to his recovery. So she'd do whatever she had to.

"Fine."

He sounded surly, which almost made her smile. At least he wasn't pretending to sleep or ignoring her.

"You received another letter from the school yesterday. They are honoring you—"

"No."

"No?" she asked, pushing the button on the bed that raised the back. The college had refitted his room with state-of-the-art medical equipment after the first stroke. And they'd hired Joy, the housekeeper, as well as two in-home nurses.

"I don't want their guilt offering," he said. His words were a lot clearer than they'd been earlier.

She adjusted the sheets over his lap, reached for his empty breakfast tray and placed it on the bed. "It's not guilt."

"How do you know?"

She knew guilt. "They're honoring you, Coach, because you brought a lot of accolades to the school."

And money.

Winning meant money and her father had been one of the winningest coaches in the history of the college.

"Where's breakfast?" he asked, slurring again.

She went to the hall and signaled Joy to bring in the food. Joy set everything up and then left.

"I want you to think about accepting this honor," Ferrin said as she ate her yogurt and fruit.

Her father had a difficult time eating but would accept no assistance from her. It was something she'd learned the hard way. He was slow lifting his right hand to his mouth and he chewed awkwardly. The left side of his face still wasn't fully functional. But he tried.

"If I take it," he said, looking up at her, his usually hazy green eyes almost clear, "then that means I'm not going back."

She didn't say anything.

He wasn't going back. But maybe believing he could would help him recover.

"I'm not sure it means that, but we can talk about it later," she said.

She should try to get some of his players to come up here and talk to him. That would cheer him up, and maybe hearing from the people he'd always wanted to spend time with would give her a key to understanding her father. A man who was still a stranger despite the past two weeks she'd spent living with him.

The doorbell rang as Joy was helping clean up the trays.

"I'll get it," Ferrin said, anxious to leave the doom of her father's room.

Hunter Caruthers rolled up to the Carmel mansion in the middle of the afternoon. He'd spent the day in the dusty archive room at his alma mater, the University of Northern California, trying to find more evidence to clear his name in the murder of his college girlfriend ten years ago.

All he'd found was that he hadn't outgrown his dust allergy. Even though his mom had always said he would. He was the youngest son of five from a big old Texas ranching family. His parents loved God, cattle, family and football. Since he'd never really loved the land the way his brothers had, Hunter had started playing football.

He'd found religion in football. He wasn't trying to aggravate anyone—especially his mom—when he said that, but he saw the world through football. He got that if no one had his back and he was wide open, he'd get the pass and then probably have to face down two or three opposing players by himself. Or he might run like all the demons in hell were chasing him and make a touchdown—become the hero of the game.

Same thing in life.

Sometimes he had to be out in the open, exposed, to make the big plays. There had been one guy who always had his back. Kingsley Buchanan. King had never wavered. He'd always stood right by his side.

They'd been arrested—and then later released—for a crime they didn't commit and that had sealed the bond between them. Guys always wanted to talk to him about his trophy-winning college career, women wanted to sleep with him because—and he was quoting here—they thought he was "dangerous," and no one wanted to really get too close to him because questions still remained.

Who had killed Stacia Krushnik? What had Kingsley and Hunter done that night? And answers seemed to be getting harder and harder to come by.

In ten years memories had faded and evidence already in short supply had disappeared.

So that was why he'd parked his Bugatti in the circle

drive of the one man who might have answers. The sun was bright—but hell, that was what living in California was all about. He'd been a bit of a hick when he'd first come here. The Pacific Ocean had awed him. Until then, he'd only ever been to the Gulf of Mexico and it didn't hold a candle to the Pacific.

Now he had a house on the beach in Malibu and when he wasn't up here in Carmel chasing down the past, he spent a lot of time on his deck watching the ocean.

He knocked on the door, pushing his sunglasses up on his head and scanning the area. The yard was nicely maintained, probably by a service. He'd never known anyone who really spent their time off working in their yard.

The door opened and an air-conditioned breeze wafted out and surrounded him. He put a friendly smile on his face.

"Hello, there," he said. The woman who'd answered the door was tall—at least five-seven—and had long curly black hair that framed her heart-shaped face. Her eyes were a brilliant blue that was almost the color of the waves he'd surfed at dawn. She had a tentative smile on her face and her lips were full. She had a long neck and wore a thin summer-weight sweater over a pair of khaki-colored shorts that reached midthigh.

Her legs…

They were long, tan, slim. And he had an uncomfortable flash of them wrapped around his hips before he shook his head and stuck his hand out.

He was here for answers, not a woman.

"Hunter Caruthers," he said. "I used to play football for Coach Gainer and I wondered if he might have some time to chat with me."

"I'm Ferrin, Coach Gainer's daughter," she said. "Come inside and we can talk."

"Coach has a daughter?"

"Yeah, he does. Be warned I'm nothing like him. Can't catch, can't throw, and it's rumored I'm allergic to all sports." She led him deeper into the house to a sunny kitchen.

"All sports?"

"As far as I can tell," she said. There was a teasing note in her voice and the slightest bit of a twang that he recognized.

As they passed the den he noticed a trophy case on one wall as well as photos of Coach Gainer with celebrities, politicians and famous alums. The one Coach had taken with Kingsley and Hunter was notably absent.

"Can I get you a drink?" she asked as she gestured to the farmhouse table in the sunny breakfast nook.

"Um… I'd like to just see Coach," Hunter said.

As cute as she was, Hunter was here on business and flirting with the coach's daughter had *dumb* written all over it.

"We have to talk first," she said.

"Lemonade talk or whiskey?"

She gave him a smile. "Lemonade. What kind of conversations have you had that require whiskey?"

He watched her as she went and filled two glasses with lemonade. "More than you want to know."

She handed him a glass and sat down across the table

from him. "Coach had a stroke earlier this year and I'm not sure what he'd be able to say to you."

A stroke?

"Is he okay?"

"The doctors say he will be. I'm here to help him recover and get back on track, but he doesn't like the medicine—never mind that. He has his good days and his bad days. I just don't know if he will talk to you or not."

Well, hell. There were times when Hunter thought he was never going to have any peace about Stacia. Maybe that was fair. Maybe the universe was leveling things out because he hadn't been able to protect her.

He didn't know. Even his mom with all her faith couldn't help him figure this one out.

"Can I try?" Hunter asked at last.

"Yes," Ferrin said.

He finished his lemonade, but noticed she didn't touch hers and that she kept staring at him.

Hell.

Did she recognize him?

"I don't know all of Coach's players. When did you play for him?"

"Ten years ago," he said. He really didn't want to mention Stacia until he had a chance to talk to Coach.

"Were you one of his famous players?" she asked.

"Sort of?"

"NFL, right? Quarterback?" she asked.

"No, that was my friend Kingsley. I was a wide receiver," he said. Apparently she didn't recognize him from the Frat House Murder scandal.

"Dad will be happy to see you. Let me take you to

him," Ferrin said, leading the way out of the kitchen. He tried to keep his eyes on the framed team portraits that lined the wall next to the curving stairs but his gaze kept skipping back to her hips. Her clothing wasn't at all come-hither, but the way she moved drew him.

She paused at the top of the stairs. "This is your team, right?"

He leaped up the last two steps and stood next to her. Yeah, that was them. Before everything had happened. He was standing next to Clive and Kingsley. God, he looked young.

And sappy. Who smiled that big for a group photo?

A guy who thought he was going to be a big-time NFL star and thought the world was his oyster, that's who.

"That was a long time ago."

She didn't respond but continued walking down the hall to the last door on the left. She opened it and gestured for him to stay in the doorway.

"Coach?" she called. "You have a visitor."

"Who is it, sunshine?" The words were slurred and as Ferrin pushed the door open further, Hunter noticed that the strong coach he remembered was now a shell of that man.

Sunshine? Coach had never seemed the type of man to give anyone a nickname. But he was seeing a different side of him.

"Hunter. He used to play football for you," Ferrin said.

"Hunter Caruthers?"

"Yes, sir, he wants to talk to you," Ferrin said. "Is that okay?"

"Yeah, I'll see him."

Ferrin went downstairs to her father's den to work while Hunter visited with the coach. She was working on an article for a small magazine that she wrote for, but the ocean just outside the French doors distracted her. So did the man upstairs. She knew few details about Hunter but his piercing green eyes and disheveled dark hair lingered in her mind as she tried to work. Instead of typing in the Word document she had opened she was tempted to launch her internet search engine and see what she could find out about him.

But she knew what she'd find. Athlete, NFL superstar. Probably had more confidence than Hercules after he'd done all of his labors. It didn't matter that she'd come here to forget her last breakup and figure out her messed-up relationship with her dad. Her mom had made an offhand comment that perhaps by not resolving the past she was repeating it by dating men who were emotionally unavailable.

Ugh.

Her mom was right but still.

Hunter…he intrigued her.

Why?

Because being attracted to a former player was easier to deal with than her dad. She knew that. Her daddy issues weren't all that exotic or hard to figure out.

It was boring here at her father's house. Especially since he wouldn't really see her except at mealtimes.

Hearing footsteps on the stairs, she quickly saved the article she'd been writing and jumped up to see who was coming.

Hunter.

He looked…well, almost angry.

"Everything okay?"

"Yes."

"You seem upset," she said.

"Upset? You don't spend a lot of time with men, do you?" he asked.

"I do," she said. "Not that it's any of your business. Why would you say that?"

"Sorry, Ferrin, I'm pissed, not upset. I guess maybe you hang out with a classier group of men than I do."

She doubted it. Stuffier maybe, but classier? She wouldn't call the psych department classy. "Pissed, eh? Why? I told you he's not really recovered yet."

"I know," Hunter said, then gave her a look that was, well, calculating. "Coach said that the college had sent everything from his office over here. I was wondering—could I take a look at it?"

"Why?"

"Well, the truth is, I needed some information I thought Coach had. He can't remember the details but I know that they used to keep track of some of that stuff."

"What stuff?" she asked.

"Videotapes from workouts at the gym and stuff from the practice field," he said. "Would you consider letting me look through the boxes?"

"What did Coach say?"

"Nothing. He didn't answer me when I asked. In fact, he didn't say much while I was in there," Hunter said.

That was strange, she thought. "I wonder why. He loves to relive the glory days."

"I'm searching for some answers about things that happened in old college football days. I was really hoping Coach could help."

The sincerity in his voice and that tightness in his stance communicated his determination. She thought it over. She had nothing else to do during the day while her father ignored her, and she'd always fancied herself a Nancy Drew type.

"Let me see what I can find out from him," Ferrin said. She wanted to double-check with Coach and make sure he was okay with her letting Hunter go through his papers. "Why don't you come back tomorrow?"

He came closer to her then and she noticed how green his eyes were. Like the fields on the first days of spring. He was handsome—there was no denying that—with his thick dark hair, classic features and lightly trimmed beard. His jaw was strong, his nose straight as a blade, his brows thick but not too thick. She wondered if he had the golden triangle proportions. He must. He was one of the handsomest men she'd ever seen.

"Couldn't you ask now?" he asked, arching one eyebrow at her. "That way we could look and then I'll take you to dinner."

"Um…dinner?"

"Yes. I'd like to get know you better, Ferrin. It's been a while since I've done anything fun. Plus I sort of owe you after being a bit of a jerk."

Fun. He thought dinner with her would be fun. She sighed. "I'll ask Coach tonight about the papers. He has physical therapy now and then he'll be napping."

"Fair enough. I shouldn't have been so pushy," Hunter said. He rubbed his hand over his chest, drawing her gaze to the way his shirt fit the muscles of his shoulders.

"So dinner. I'll pick you up at six," he said.

"You will? Shouldn't you ask me?" She wasn't sure what he was up to. It was clear that he'd changed gears when he realized she wouldn't be budged. Even knowing he was probably trying to get something from her wasn't enough to make her say no.

She hadn't been out on a date in a long time. She'd broken up with Roger before Christmas, and really that relationship had been dying for at least three months before then. If nothing else, going out with Hunter would provide her some distraction from all the gloom that seemed to cling to this house, and to her while she was living in it.

"Apologies," he said. "Will you have dinner with me tonight?"

She tipped her head to the side, pretending to think it over.

"I guess so."

"You guess so?"

"You said it yourself. I'm used to classy," she said. Even though she wasn't. But she didn't want to make this too easy for him. With that pretty face and muscled body, she doubted he ever had to work hard to get a date.

"Oh, I'll give you classy, Ferrin," he said. "You just wait and see. I'll be back at six."

"I'll be ready at six thirty," she said.

He threw his head back and laughed. "You're a minx."

Doubtful. But she was tired of the same-old, same-old, and Hunter promised something different.

"Six thirty then. Dress classy."

"As if I'd do anything else," she said, leading him down the hall. She opened the front door and leaned back against it as he brushed past her. He stopped and leaned down, putting his hand on the bottom of her chin.

Dinner suddenly seemed like more than just a break in the routine. She suspected he might want something from her but that was okay. She wanted something from him, too. A chance to remember she was young and single. Maybe make a memory in California that wasn't laced with guilt and disappointment.

Two

Rocky Point Restaurant was famous in Carmel-by-the-Sea for its views of the Big Sur coastline. And since Ferrin had mentioned not being out of the house since she'd arrived, Hunter thought she'd enjoy being around other people. Plus, if he was completely honest, he really didn't trust himself alone with her.

He might have gone to the Gainer house to see Coach and get answers, but tonight he was torn. Right now, his focus was on seeing Ferrin and a part of him—granted, a small part—didn't even care if she let him see Coach's boxes from his office.

She wore her thick, black curly hair down and it brushed the tops of her shoulders, which were left bare by her bohemian-style top. The blouse was a sea-blue color and she'd paired it with slim-fitting white jeans that made her legs seem even longer than they had earlier in those shorts. She had on heels, which made her only a few inches shorter than his six-two frame.

And as they walked from the parking lot to the restaurant, he was aware of people watching them. For a moment he forget he was Hunter Caruthers, famous for being accused of the Frat House Murder, and pretended people just noticed a good-looking couple.

But as soon as they got closer, people turned away and gave them a wide berth.

He cursed under his breath.

"What?"

"Nothing. I thought going out would put you at ease but I might have misjudged this. Everyone here knows me."

She put her hand on his arm, her touch light and delicate. "That doesn't matter. They don't know the real you."

"You don't either," he pointed out as he pulled her to one side before they entered the restaurant. "I wouldn't blame you if you demanded I take you home."

"You don't know me either, Hunter. I'm not one to bug out on a date before it's even started. I can handle a little gossip," she said. "Are you one of those bad-boy players in the NFL?"

"Not really. I mean I do date pretty women and have a few rushing records, but I don't see myself as a bad boy." He wondered if she'd already Googled him and knew the scandal that followed him around like a dark cloud, driving him away from anything good. Damn, he was getting dramatic. It was just that ten years was too long to be on the run from the past. Even his dad, who made laconic seem chatty, had said maybe it was time to get answers, to find out what had really happened.

"Who would see himself as a bad boy?" she asked with a wink. "But you should know that no matter what else happens between us, I'm not someone for you to toy with."

He reached around her to open the door. She entered the restaurant and walked over to the hostess.

He saw Coach's inner steel in Ferrin. And she didn't know who he was, which was reassuring and a bit worrying. He'd have to tell her. It had been a long time since he'd had to do that. In fact, most everyone he met already knew the stories if not the facts. He should come clean with her but from past experience, he knew once he told her about his connection to the Frat House Murder, she'd freeze up on him.

"Party of two?"

"I made a reservation," he told the hostess. "Hunter Caruthers."

The hostess nodded and led them to a table that overlooked the craggy cliffs that led down to the sandy beaches of Big Sur. He held Ferrin's chair the way his mama had taught him to before sitting down himself.

They ordered drinks and dinner before Hunter remembered this wasn't just a date. He had invited her tonight to soften her up and get her to give him a glimpse at Coach's old files even though her old man wasn't in an agreeable mood.

"So…"

"You want to see my dad's old office stuff. I know.

And I'm thinking about it. But my dad and I aren't on the best of terms and doing something blatant to anger him without a good reason makes no sense to me."

"Fair enough, ma'am. But what if I can convince you that he won't mind?"

"I'd say you're relying a little too heavily on that good old boy charm. I'm immune to that Texas 'aw shucks' attitude."

He threw his head back and laughed. At Coach's house, Ferrin had seemed…well, *timid* didn't feel like the right word to describe this feisty woman. But she had been subdued earlier.

"What can I do to convince you?" he asked.

"Tell me something about Hunter that the world doesn't know."

"So nothing to do with football then," he said.

"Yeah, nothing to do with football," she said.

He couldn't understand her attitude toward the sport. He'd always thought it would be great to grow up with a coach as a father. His own dad really only cared about the cattle, the land…their family legacy. But Hunter had never understood it.

"Why don't you like football?" he asked.

She took a sip of her wine and glanced out toward the setting sun. He noticed the burnished copper in her dark hair and for the first time realized it was layered with different colors. The wind blew, stirring the strands against her face, and she put her glass down and looked over at him. Her blue eyes were serious and almost sad.

"I could never compete with football or the players in

my dad's eyes. So I didn't even try. It's not that I don't like football it's just—"

"You hate it," he said.

"*Hate* is really a strong word."

"Not for a passionate woman," he said. "I get it. I feel that way about cattle. My family has a big spread in the Hill Country and my brothers all love the land. Or most of them do—one of my brothers is a surgeon. But damned if I didn't hate ranching from…well, from birth, I imagine."

"So you played football?"

"Well, ma'am, I am from Texas."

"I could tell," she said.

"What about you? I'm pretty sure I heard a bit of twang when you talk."

"I teach at UT Austin."

"Let me guess. Literature," he said.

"Wrong. I'm a psychology lecturer."

"Wrong? Good thing we didn't wager on it," he said.

She laughed. "Good thing. I bet you're not used to losing."

The mantle of the past fell heavy on his shoulders. He had only really lost once and he'd done it bigger than life when Stacia had been killed and he'd been blamed for her murder.

"No one gets used to losing," he said.

She put her hand on his where it lay on the table and squeezed. She was very different from the coach, who'd always told them to shake it off. She was empathetic, and a part of him knew he could play on that. Get her to give him what he wanted. Another part wanted not to have to play games with her. But he was a player. He always had been.

"I'm sorry, Hunter. Tell me again why you need to see my father's papers and effects."

He turned his hand over in hers, rubbed his thumb over the back of her knuckles while he thought about it. If he went for the hard sell now she'd pull back. He needed…he needed her to feel important. As if he was here for her.

And he was, as long as she had access to the information he needed to clear up the past. But something didn't feel right about that. Maybe this date was a mistake because getting to know Ferrin was making him feel as if using her was wrong.

"I'm here to finally solve the Frat House Murder case. And clear my name once and for all."

She put her hands in her lap and linked them together tightly. A chill spread down her spine as she stared at the man whom she'd been dining with. *Murderer.* The word echoed in her head but a part of her had a hard time reconciling that with the man she'd come to know throughout the evening.

Her throat was dry and she knew she had to say something. He watched her carefully but she had no idea how to respond to what he'd just said.

"Um…"

"Yeah, it's kind of a mood breaker," he said. "At first I'd thought you might have recognized my name but then it became clear you didn't."

"No. I really don't follow sports or my dad's teams that closely," she said. "So tell me what happened."

"Okay, I don't know where to start."

"The beginning is probably a good idea," she said. She was still trying to wrap her mind around the fact that he'd been accused of murder. He didn't feel threatening to her at all. "Were you arrested?"

"Yes. But we were released on bond and charges were never brought," he said. "That's why it's so important that I get a look at your dad's files."

"Do you think Coach had something to do with the murders?" she asked.

He shrugged. "No, I don't. But we are missing the videotapes from the gym and that's where the attack on Stacia took place. I think they might be in your dad's files. He kept everything."

"Yes, he did. He reviewed those tapes every night when I was with him. What makes you think he has tapes from the gym? I remember seeing practice footage," she said. She was trying to understand what Hunter thought he'd find.

"And he gave me and the other players notes the next day. He'd tell me if I was slacking off on the middle reps on a specific weight machine. I know he reviewed the gym tapes too."

"It's a lot to think about," she said at last. She wanted to help Hunter but if her father said no, she wasn't going to rock the boat with him by going behind his back. That wasn't her way.

"Want to take a walk?" Hunter asked. "Unless you don't feel safe with me."

She looked over at him, saw the uncertainty in his gaze and felt a tug at her heart. She'd been accused in middle school of cheating on a test; she hadn't cheated and her mom had gotten the teacher to change her grade but the other students all believed she had cheated. Though it wasn't the same as Hunter's situation, she remembered what it had been like when she'd gone to the honor society meetings and people would stare at her as if she didn't belong there.

"I feel safe with you," she admitted.

Hunter paid the bill and led the way down to the beach. For a man who had once been accused of murder, Hunter was charming in a self-deprecating way, Ferrin noted as they walked along the beach. The breeze blew her hair and the only sound that accompanied them was the waves crashing on the shore. He wanted her dad's information, and given how little she cared about it, she was tempted to just give it to him. But this was the Gainer legacy. It was all that her father had left—and there was something in those boxes of practice tapes, game-day films and old files that her father was afraid of.

She doubted there was anything in the files that would help Hunter. What could her father have possibly known about a coed's death and not shared with the cops? But at the same time…she liked Hunter. There was something about him that was different from all the other men she'd met.

He was a jock but not like the others. He was one of her father's favored honorary sons but he didn't look through her. Didn't make her feel as if she was too bookish to warrant his attention. And maybe it was just that he was good-looking and paying attention to her. That couldn't be ruled out. She might be serious and pretend to be sophisticated but she wasn't dead.

"What are you thinking? You've been glancing at me from the corner of your eye for the last few minutes," Hunter said, drawing her to a stop near a rocky outcropping.

"Nothing," she said. *Right!* As if she was going to tell him that she was contemplating his attractiveness.

"Sweetheart, I know you think I'm a dumb jock—"

"Never. There is nothing dumb about you, Hunter," she said, glancing out at the endless cycling of the waves and realizing that was the problem. If he'd been like every other player on her dad's team, then she'd have said *thanks for dinner, I'm outta here.* But he wasn't.

"Aw, shucks, ma'am."

"Can it, Caruthers. You know you're charming. You play that card when you think it will work to your advantage."

"Is it working?"

"Maybe. I haven't decided yet," she said.

He turned so that his body was closer to hers. He wasn't touching her but it wasn't that hard to imagine his hands on her shoulders, pulling her closer... Ugh. She needed—him. She needed for once to be in her dad's world and in control. And Hunter wanted something from her. Why shouldn't she take something from him?

She lifted her hand, skimmed her fingers along the neat beard on his jaw. His facial hair was soft and smooth to her touch. Cool from the breeze that was wrapping around them. The heat of his skin radiated upward, making her fingers tingle.

"What is going on in that beautiful head of your?" he asked, his voice a low rumble. She closed her eyes so she could try to make a "wise decision" but her hormones and her gut said too late. That ship had sailed as soon as he'd tried to back out of the date because of what strangers might think of her for eating with him.

She opened her eyes and was unnerved to see he was watching her. That his green-eyed stare was fixed on her. Just waiting.

He'd been judged many times in his life. She understood that from the stillness in his body and in his gaze. He was waiting for her to reject him, walk away. But he wasn't cowering.

"How do you do it?"

"Do what?"

"Live with it. Live with the attention and not go nuts."

"It's been hard. But the truth is, I'm innocent. That's what gets me through. That and Kingsley. He and I both know the truth of that night."

She nodded.

"I'm not sure about letting you have carte blanche with Dad's videos and files," she said. "But I don't want you to walk out of my life. Not yet."

The side of his mouth lifted in a slight grin. "I'm listening."

"I want…that sounds so selfish, doesn't it?"

"Not at all. I told you what I wanted. Why shouldn't you have what you want?" he asked.

His voice was silky smooth, much the way she imagined the devil must sound when he was leading some poor sinner to her doom. But this didn't feel like doom. The excitement in her stomach felt more like anticipation. As if she was alive for the first time in a really long time. As though she was living instead of just existing.

And it was too tempting to pass up.

"I want a chance to get to know the man. But if you are just here because of Dad, then tell me now. I think there is a spark between us. I want to explore it but I don't want to bribe you into dating me by holding Dad's files out as a carrot." Instant attraction, falling in love at first sight; she was too practical to believe in those things, but in this moment with the half-moon hanging above them, it felt as though there was magic in the air.

He cupped her face in his hands. They were large and surprisingly smooth against her skin. He tipped her head back slightly so that their eyes met and he looked into hers with an intensity that made her shiver. What was he looking for?

"No bribe needed," he said, lowering his head and kissing her.

She smelled of some sweet flowery perfume and the sea. Dinner had been interesting. It had changed something that he didn't think could ever be changed and now she was being so sweet. Telling him everything he needed to do to get what he wanted.

Just be smooth, he thought. But then he heard his assistant Asia's voice in his head. *Don't be a douche.*

He rubbed his thumb over Ferrin's bottom lip. Her

breath came out in a rush. Tiny trembles coursed through her body, and if he weren't touching her, standing this close to her, he wouldn't have known it.

There she was again, the shy woman he'd met at the coach's house. Not the feisty woman who had boldly gone to dinner with an infamous football player. It was the contradictions that drew him. He knew that.

He hated things that were easy to pigeonhole.

"Are you kissing me or not?" she said.

He laughed.

"I am… I just don't want to make the wrong move. My conscience—"

"I thought you were a player. I bet you blow through women like they are disposable tissues."

"You're not disposable, are you?" he asked. He knew she wasn't. "You just changed the dynamic between us. You don't want to bribe me into a relationship and I need to make damned sure I don't take the easy path. That's what got me into trouble the last time."

She took a few steps away from him and began walking back toward the restaurant and her car. He knew he'd screwed up. He had a gift for it.

He took two steps toward her and caught her in his arms, softly, gently, the way he would a pass that was just out of reach. He cradled her softly and spun her, lifting her off her feet.

"What are you doing?"

"Fixing a mistake," he said.

He had to stop thinking.

Hadn't Coach been the one to say that the only way to improve his game was to listen to his instincts?

He brought his mouth down on hers, not hard, because he had some self-control left. But softly. He rubbed her lips with his and tasted the coffee she'd drunk after dinner as she opened her mouth.

She twined her arms around his neck and tilted her head to the side, and suddenly he wasn't worrying about the mistakes he'd made or the reasons why he was kissing her.

He couldn't not kiss Ferrin. She was everything that he wanted and nothing that he felt he could allow himself to have. For the first time since Stacia…he felt something for a woman. Maybe it was the fact that Kingsley had settled down with Gabi de la Cruz or maybe—God, please—it was that he was close to finding out what had really happened to Stacia.

Maybe it was his usual need to conquer or maybe it was something more. Only time would tell.

Right now he didn't need to know anything other than how soft and cold Ferrin's fingers felt against the side of his face. How the way she kept running her fingertip over his light beard sent tingles down his neck and chest and straight to his groin.

How she softened against him and let him take all of her weight as the kiss deepened. He pulled his head back and looked down at her. Her lips were parted, her eyes half-closed, and there was a slight flush on her creamy skin.

He could push a little more right now. It wouldn't take much for either of them to fall into bed together, but he wanted more than one night. He knew games were won by plays and downs. Ten yards at a time.

Sometimes faking out the other team was the way to gain more yards.

He set her on her feet. Tangled his hands in that thick gorgeous hair of hers and kissed her again even though he had decided not to. But really, what man could resist her, with her swollen lips and her sweet face looking up at him as if she wanted…well, what he wanted.

Damn.

Things just got complicated.

He couldn't control himself around her.

When the hell had that happened? He'd always been a man of control. But with Ferrin…

He stepped away from her, turned his back to her and stared out at the sea with his hands on his hips. It had been a long six months since he'd had a lover… maybe that was it.

Please let that be it. The reason why he was having a hard time resisting her. A hard time not going back to her and scooping her up in his arms, carrying her someplace semiprivate and making damned sure that she didn't lose that look in her eyes.

But he couldn't.

Ten yards at a time.

Damn.

These ten yards hurt.

"Hunter?"

"I just don't want to be that guy."

"What guy?" she asked, walking over to him.

He noticed the strand of her hair that brushed over her swollen lips and wanted to touch it. Maybe wrap it around his fingers. But he knew if he touched her again he wouldn't stop.

"The one you think I am," he said. "The *bad boy* NFL player who has a different woman every week. I want to be more."

"Well, that guy, the player, probably wouldn't be here with me. Already things are different," she said. "It must be hard for you to let your guard down."

"It is. And I want something from you, Ferrin. Despite the money and the silver spoon upbringing, I'm the kind of person who isn't above using whatever means I have to get what I want. I want to be better than that with you. But I'm not sure that I can resist the temptation of you."

"I'm a temptation?"

"Dammit, woman."

"Sorry, I'm not going to apologize for that. I've never been the type of woman to tempt a man or to make him want to be better."

"I find that hard to believe," he said.

"I'm invisible, Hunter."

Never.

Three

In the clear light of day, waking up alone in his bed, Hunter wished he'd just brought Ferrin home with him last night. He rolled over, punching the pillow next to him, and then forced himself up and out of bed.

He was working a plan. He dropped to the floor and did fifty push-ups. His dad had said that staying focused was the only way to move past the tragedy. That's what his family referred to Stacia's death as. He knew they meant well.

They thought he and King should leave the matter in the past, but both of them knew they couldn't. He finished his push-ups, got dressed for running and dialed King's number as he went down the stairs.

"Dude, it's early."

"But I know Conner had you up early." Kingsley's

son was two so he didn't sleep late. There had even been times when Hunter had been woken by the kid, who also happened to be his godson. They were close and since Kingsley traveled so much, Conner had learned to use his iPad to FaceTime Hunter. Conner felt he could call at all hours to tell Hunter things such as when he read a new book at bedtime or saw something cool in the night sky.

"He did. That's why I'm complaining. Just got him off to his playdate and Gabi and I are finally alone."

Hunter laughed. "Sorry, dude. I'll keep this short. Coach has had two strokes and a heart attack. He wouldn't really talk to me or give me permission to go through his stuff. I'm working another angle."

"What angle?"

"Coach's daughter."

"Coach has a daughter?"

"Yeah. She's…smart and funny."

"Pretty?"

Pretty? "She's got eyes the color of the water around Aruba—remember that old wreck we went scuba diving in?"

"Yes."

"Well, her eyes are that color."

"Dang, Hunter, you sound—"

"Like an idiot," he said. "I know. But she's different, King. Not what I expected."

"So you're working her to get to the files?"

Was he? He had a plan. Seduce her and get what he wanted. Last night the plan had been screwed up by the wine and her defiant attitude in eating with him while gossips looked on. But this morning he was back on track.

"Yeah. It's complicated, though."

"Women always are. You want me to talk to her. That way you don't have—"

"No. I'll do this. When have I ever asked you to do anything for me?"

"Never. We each carry our own weight but we're teammates. We're like brothers, Hunter. I'm here if you need me."

"Thanks, King. Same. I got this," he said. "I'm going for a run and then...how do you feel about hosting Ferrin and me for dinner?"

"Why?"

"I want her to know you and me. To understand that we're not asking for the files for any reason other than to clear our names."

"Okay. I'll check with Gabi and let you know when we can do it."

He hung up with King and went for his run. The mountain paths he ran on out here in California were very different from the "hills" near where he'd grown up in Texas. Back home, they had gently rolling slopes; he never used to strain when he went uphill the way he did here.

He rounded the last bend and ran up to his front door past a car he didn't recognize. He stopped short on the bottom step that led to his porch. His interior designer had furnished the patio with two large California cedar deck chairs.

Ferrin sat in one of them. She had a foam cup in one

hand, her sunglasses were pushed up on her head and she had her legs delicately crossed. She wore a pair of faded jeans—they looked soft. She had on a pair of flip-flops and her painted toenails were a deep red color.

"Hello."

"Morning," she said. "I hope you don't mind but I thought maybe we could spend the day together."

He ran through his schedule in his head. He had a meeting with his assistant this morning and a fundraising briefing in the afternoon with a local small-town peewee football league that he was sponsoring. They needed gear for the league.

"I've got a couple meetings, but otherwise I'm free," he said. "Want to come inside? We can figure this out."

"You work?"

He gave her a look over his shoulder. "My dad would disagree because I'm not out on the ranch helping him. But yeah, I work."

"What do you do?"

"I run a foundation that encourages kids to participate in sports and funds sporting groups in low-income areas. Trying to level the playing field."

"Wow," she said. "I had no idea."

"I know. My involvement in the foundation is low-key. It's easier to give away the money if we don't associate me with it."

"That's not fair. You were cleared of any wrongdoing back in college. I'd think that having a former NFL player would be something they'd publicize."

"But that's not how the world sees it," he said, unlocking the door. Still, his work with the foundation made him feel a little less empty after everything that had happened surrounding Stacia's death. "You coming in? You can wait on the deck in the back or in the kitchen while I take a quick shower."

"I'll wait on the deck. I like being outside. We don't have to do this today," she said.

"I want to. Spending the day with you is what we need."

"We?"

"Yes, so you can trust that I'm not going to do something to hurt your dad. And so that I can remember the man I used to be."

He went up the stairs two at a time. In the shower he pretended that her presence in his home fit his plan, but she'd thrown him. She was a linebacker he'd missed when he was running his route, and though she seemed like a lightweight, she was capable of bringing him down before he reached the end zone.

Ferrin had no real agenda when she'd decided to come to Hunter's house. She must be here to try to figure out if she should give Hunter access to her father's files. To get answers.

Or at least that was what she told herself.

It wasn't because of the kiss that had plagued her dreams all night. Or the fact that for the first time she thought she might be experiencing lust. Real lust. Not the kind that she could explain away as mating instinct or her biological clock. She wanted Hunter. There was nothing logical about it. It was all white-hot lust. They had nothing in common; it was just the way he looked.

That big, muscly body of his and the fact that he was focusing all of his attention on her. She wished it bothered her but it didn't.

She was a thinker. She had never been attracted to any of her dad's players…at least not since she'd turned eighteen and started to make a life for herself as an adult. She prided herself on being above her animal instincts, and one dinner with Hunter had made her question all of that.

One dinner.

Why was she here?

"You look way too serious for this gorgeous sunny morning," Hunter said, stepping out onto the porch. He'd changed from his running clothes into a white linen summer suit paired with a pastel-colored shirt. On anyone else it would have looked as if he was trying too hard, but on Hunter it fit. His hair was artfully styled, his beard neatly trimmed and he smelled fresh and clean.

"We're not all used to dancing our way through life."

"Ah. So you're tasting a little bit of regret this morning," he said.

"Why would I be? We didn't do anything last night."

"Is that the problem?" he asked, sitting down next to her in one of the deck chairs.

"I don't know," she said. Honesty—it was one of the tenets of her life. "Maybe."

"Me, too," he said. "But we can always rectify that. We would never have been able to fix it if we had moved too fast and had regrets this morning. Would you like to join me for breakfast or have you eaten?"

"Breakfast would be great. What did you have in mind?" she asked, getting to her feet. In her mind she had a checklist. Kind of like when she did a psych evaluation at work. Her mother had told her more than once that relationships wouldn't work if she filtered through theories, but she really had no other way to figure out what made Hunter tick.

"I'm meeting my assistant at a little diner off the Five. She works in my main office in Malibu and is driving up to give me some papers to sign and other stuff. So it's a forty-minute drive."

"Sounds good. Dad's not expecting me until dinnertime."

"Have you thought any more about letting me see his files?" Hunter asked.

"Of course. That's why I'm here."

"Oh, I thought you were here because we shared one hot kiss last night."

"Well, I'm curious about that, too," she said. Then realized she probably sounded like an idiot.

He watched her.

She had an uncomfortable feeling that she was being played and wondered if she shouldn't just tell him no to the files and see what happened next. He shook his head.

"Sorry about that. Sometimes when I see what I want it makes me intense."

"It's fine."

"No, it's not. I'm not pressuring you at all. I just was trying to see if I should drop my interest in the files. If that would be enough to make you believe that the kiss we shared last night was real. And not part of a play I'm making," he said.

But he was a master playmaker.

This was complicated. But she'd made up her mind. He'd read her…maybe a little too well, but he was smart enough to realize using the lust between them to manipulate her wasn't going to be the easiest way to get what he wanted.

She followed him out of his house. They drove up the Five. Hunter was a relaxed driver who had no problems keeping the conversation going. He told her about his best friend Kingsley getting engaged to his college girlfriend and about his godson, Conner, who tried to FaceTime them while they were driving.

"You're close to them," she said.

"King is like a brother to me. Closer actually."

Suddenly everything about Hunter became clear. He'd do whatever he had to in order to see her dad's files. She didn't doubt that he may have toyed with seducing her and she didn't know if he'd really dropped it, but she knew the stakes were high for him.

Interesting.

The shallow playboy had real connections. Ones she hadn't guessed at before, and keeping him from her father's files was going to be harder than she'd imagined.

Hunter's meeting with Asia, his assistant, went smoothly. He'd texted her to say he was bringing a woman and to keep her smart-ass comments to herself. His assistant was very good at her job but she liked to sass him all the time.

"I like her. She doesn't let you get away with anything," Ferrin said when they were back in the car.

"I know. I hired her because she was the only one who didn't ask to see my Super Bowl ring," he said. "She couldn't care less about football but she loves kids and grew up in a rough neighborhood so gets that kids having something fun and productive to do is important."

"I could see that. I thought you were one of those rich boys who just took what he wanted and damn the consequences," she said.

"Well, I'm a man, not a boy," he said, giving Ferrin a long level look. Maybe he was moving too slow.

Desire flashed in her pretty blue eyes as she took him in with a glance. "I know you're a man."

Good enough. He wanted her to be aware of him. "Do you surf?"

"Do I look like I surf?" she countered. "Actually, I'm not very sporty."

"How was that, growing up with Coach?"

"Horrible. I can't catch a football, which used to enrage him. I'm okay at running but I don't like it and I can swim but that isn't a 'real' sport, according to him."

"I can teach you to catch," Hunter said. "I'm really good at it."

"I figured, since you're a wide receiver. I'm smart that way."

"Yeah, you are. How about paddleboarding?"

"How about driving up the coast and eating lunch at this restaurant that I know? Or taking a walk on the beach?"

"I like it. But you're never going to really know me unless you see me in action," he said. When he talked he got into trouble. He said the wrong thing, and with Ferrin when he was being so careful to watch his every move, he didn't want to chance it.

"I want to know the man, not the player, Hunter. Talking will do," she said.

"You're right, I'm happy to do that but in return you will do something with me."

"Football?" she asked. The dread in her voice amused him.

"It's not like I'm asking you to outrun zombies."

"I think I'd prefer that," she said. "I'm going to level with you. I never liked football and I know it's because my dad loved it more than anything—and anyone—else."

Hunter put his hand on her shoulder and squeezed it gently. "My dad is that way about the land."

"The land?"

"Our family has a ranch that is generations old and when other families left and went to Dallas or moved on to oil, we kept cattle. It's the only thing that Dad really understands. Football is okay for a man to watch on the weekends but to make a living at it, well, in his mind, that's a lazy man's path."

"Football is at the crux of both our lives," she said.

"See, we're not so different after all," he said, but they were different. He'd made his peace with his father. He'd always gone home in the off-season when he'd still been playing, and more frequently now. He did the early morning chores with his father. They'd gotten past the differences from their past. Ferrin hadn't found that yet with Coach. Could Hunter do that for her? Mend that relationship?

Why did he want to?

Because he wanted her and was going to use her anyway, he thought. He needed to justify his actions to himself. To somehow make it seem as though it was okay for him to use her, to take her and the information he needed.

"Okay."

"Okay?"

"You can look through Dad's files. But... I'll go through them with you," she said.

Score.

But it didn't feel like a touchdown. He felt as if he'd gotten the points due to something sly. A cheat.

"When you're ready," he said. "I still want to teach you to catch and spend the day with you."

She gave him a long look from those gorgeous eyes of hers. And he realized there was much more to her than he'd noticed before.

"Waiting isn't going to make me think you want to be with me more than you want to see the files," she said.

"I know. But it will make me feel better that you are letting me see them," he said.

"For a badass that's not really a tough attitude."

"The last time I put football before a woman it ended badly, Ferrin, but I need to make sure my conscience is clean on this."

"Are you talking about Stacia? I want to know more

about that. But I know it must be hard for you to talk about it," she said.

Ferrin was right; he didn't want to tell her the painful memories of Stacia's death, how he'd broken up with her the very night she was murdered and had felt guilty about it ever since. But he knew he was going to have to. Only by talking about the past could he believe that she would understand why those files were so important.

"Definitely," he said. "But not today. Today is about the present."

She gave him another look, and to his guilty soul it seemed she read the truth buried beneath what he hoped was charm. "Fine. But you know it's hard to move forward when you are carrying the weight of the past."

He rubbed the back of his neck and nodded. "I'm very well acquainted with that fact."

"It's okay. This is only our second date. I was just trying to be helpful," she said. "Occupational hazard, I guess."

"Right, psychology professor. Why teach instead of practice?" he asked.

"Teaching suits me. My parents are teachers."

"I guess coaching is teaching, isn't it?"

"I meant my stepdad, but coaching can be considered teaching, as well."

She didn't include Coach when she talked about her parents. That was interesting, and he wanted to know more. He would take today to learn about her and when he got her home he'd tell her the whole truth about Stacia and the past.

Four

The beach wasn't too crowded in the middle of the day as they walked down it. Though she'd said she wanted to talk, she wasn't too sure now. Hunter seemed to have no barriers and she didn't really want to know the raw, broken man underneath the sexy exterior. She'd reacted to him on an intimate level and it would be much easier to just kiss him, take him to her bed and then show him the door.

But his pain was real to her. Observed in the quiet moments when he thought she wasn't watching him. There was a palpable drive to it, as well. The woman in her wanted to comfort him.

Sex would do that, she thought.

Lust. It truly had been a long time since she'd met a man who just plain turned her on the way he did.

Emotions. These emotions weren't comfortable for her. Give her a nice, calm feeling of indifference—that was really all she wanted.

"What's the deal with you and your dad?" Hunter asked as he stopped to look out at the sea.

"I'm not sure what you mean," she said. This was a mistake. Just go buy a football and let him throw it to her. That was what she should have done. But instead she'd wanted to talk.

Her mom would be...understanding. She'd probably be able to offer some insight that Ferrin herself was missing. She wondered if he'd let her call a time-out on their day date to call her mom.

She started laughing at how ridiculous that thought was.

"You okay?"

"No. No, I'm not. I suggested this to get to know you better but you turned the tables on me and suddenly I realized I don't want to let you any closer. I don't want to get to know a man who loves a sport I hate. A man who wants something from the father I barely know. A man who makes me aware of myself as a woman. I am so used to being in control of myself and my environment."

Hunter put his hands up, shoulder-level, and cocked his head to the side. "I wanted to play football. It's quick and physical and neither of us would have to do much thinking while we were playing."

"Except I would. I can't catch."

"I think you can."

"Past history would say otherwise," she said, knowing she was letting him lead her away from the fact that she'd just sort of laid her soul bare and he'd scooted around it.

She had to remember that. The fact that he had ignored the emotion she'd shown him and ducked behind football. He was an expert at blocking.

"It's all in your head," he said. "Just start thinking 'I'm an expert receiver.'"

She looked at him. As if she cared if she could catch a football. Well, okay, she did. It was the one thing that was a concrete reminder to her and her father that she wasn't the child he wanted or thought he deserved.

"I'll try," she said.

"Listen, I don't think we can do the big, serious talk thing. It's just not my style and it makes me really uncomfortable. Want to try surfing?"

"Surfing?"

"Yeah, we could grab some wet suits and boards," he suggested. "I bet I'll spill my guts when we are out there."

Doubtful. "Counteroffer."

"I'm listening."

"We rent paddleboards instead. Didn't you say that was one of our options earlier? I know a great cove just over there," she said, gesturing to it. "And as a bonus I can actually do it without wiping out."

"Accepted. Where do we rent the boards?" he asked.

She led him to the shop that she'd been using. They both purchased bathing suits and paid for their board rentals. She dashed into the dressing room to get changed and realized that she was excited.

Forget about lust; it would wane over time. She was just thrilled to be here with Hunter. And that hadn't happened for her with a man in a really long time.

She stored her clothes in the locker provided by the establishment and stepped outside to find Hunter chatting with a group of men. He said something to them and they waved as he walked away.

Fans.

His life was different from hers. He was a celebrity, which was easy to forget when they were alone. But it was important for her to remember. It must be difficult for him to balance the adulation from the fans who loved him and the condemnation of the people who still weren't sure he hadn't killed his girlfriend. She wasn't looking for entrée into that type of life or was even sure that was what she wanted.

"Lookin' good, lady," Hunter said.

"You're not so bad yourself," she said, but being flirty didn't feel right to her.

He wore a pair of board shorts that rode low on his hips. His chest muscles appeared firm even from a distance. Her fingers tingled with the need to touch him.

"Why are you out with me?" she asked after a moment.

"You were waiting on my front step when I got home. My mama raised me to be gentlemanly," he said.

One thing she was coming to know about Hunter was he spent a lot of time deflecting any honest answer with humor or sarcasm.

"I'm serious. You're a famous person. You should be with a model or some other gorgeous woman."

He put his hand on her waist and drew her closer to him. "I am with a gorgeous woman, and I'm not famous at the end of the day. I'm just Hunter. A guy who used to play football and is now here with you."

She wanted to take his words at face value, and even though she was pretty sure there was more to the story than he'd said, for today she was happy to ignore it.

It was only their second date. No matter how many times she reminded herself of that fact, it still felt as though they had much more between them.

Hunter followed Ferrin as she paddled out into the ocean toward the cove she knew about. He hadn't wanted to tell her the truth that for every group of fans who remembered him from his playing days there were at least two groups of people who remembered him from being arrested and accused of murder.

He had stayed away from dating seriously, because what woman deserved to be under that kind of spotlight?

They paddled for about an hour before she led the way back to shore into a private cove. There were a young mom with her two kids and some seabirds but otherwise they had the beach to themselves.

They carried their boards out of the water and set them on the ground. "That was nice."

"I'm glad. It's the kind of nonsport I enjoy."

"Why do you call it a nonsport?"

"Coach. He always said I wasn't an athlete and I guess I believe him. I like yoga and rock climbing and stuff like this."

"You know he's not right," Hunter said. "You're plenty athletic, honey."

Coach wasn't a very good parent, Hunter thought, and it surprised him. He was seeing a different side of the man he thought he knew. On the field Coach had always nurtured his players.

Hunter reached for Ferrin's hand. He had said as much as he could. *The good stuff.* The stuff about Stacia that made him seem like a decent guy. Nothing about the boy who'd broken up with her just hours before she was found dead. The guy who wanted to be "free" so he could graduate and get as much NFL tail as he could. That guy didn't deserve closure. That guy was probably living in the karma he'd created. If he fixed it…maybe then he'd have some peace with the past.

If only it were that simple. But a part of him wanted it to be. A big part of him wanted to be like the other people who visited the beach, carefree and enjoying a day in the sun. Not carrying around the burden of not meeting parental expectations as Ferrin was, or the chains of the past as he was.

They wouldn't really be able to do that but they could try.

"Honey? I don't believe I gave you leave to call me honey."

"Would you prefer *baby*?" he asked.

She flushed and bit her lower lip. "How about you stick to my given name for now."

She moved through life cautiously; she was all rushing yards and strategic huddling behind her offensive line. He wanted to warn her that wasn't the way to win the game, but he suspected the strategy worked well for her.

"Tell me about your name," he said. "Ferrin is a bit unusual."

He joined their hands together and noticed how well they fit, her longish fingers braiding nicely with his. He tugged her into motion, walking along the line where the tide swept onto the sand.

"It is different. I never purchased a souvenir with my name on it growing up," she said.

"Same. There weren't a lot of key chains with Hunter on them," he said. "So are you named after someone?"

"Yes. It's my great-grandfather's middle name on my father's side. It was his mother's maiden name. Usually Ferrin gets buried as a middle name or something like that. But my mother, whose name is Jennifer, thought her own name was too common and wanted me to have a unique name."

He smiled.

"A unique name for a one-of-a-kind woman," he said.

"I wish you knew me well enough to believe that," she said.

He paused. He kept forgetting how serious she was. How deep that mind of hers ran and how she saw past some of the flashy things he'd been throwing out for so long that he sometimes forgot they weren't real. He wished he hadn't said that to her. Not now. He should have waited until he knew her better.

"I will," he said, the words a promise to himself.

"Don't. Let's just—"

"Stop selling me short, Ferrin," he said.

"Was that what I was doing?" she asked. There was something fragile about her as they stood there in the sun with the surfers out on the waves and the kids busily building sandcastles on the beach.

"Yes. Why do you do that?" he asked.

She tugged her hand free and wrapped her arm around her waist. A shy woman. Not the one who'd driven to his house and sat in the sun waiting for him.

"Promises are easy to make. Just a couple of words today and then forgotten. Maybe that's what this day should be. Just a bit of fun until we figure out if I can go behind my father's back and give you what you want. But another part of me will want to believe it. Want to see you as a man who is more than just empty words that the sea breeze swept away. If you aren't I'll have to deal with that," she said.

Fair enough. He'd been many different things to people and he knew that more than once he'd failed them. He was human and fallible.

"We all make mistakes, but that doesn't mean that everything I say is a pass fake. I might be focused on cleaning up my past but that doesn't mean I'm not going to try to have a decent future. I'm tired of cleaning up the bad juju."

"I know we all make mistakes. Especially me. It's easy to stand here next to you and imagine saying, 'Hey, Dad, I'm going to let Hunter have those boxes,' but when I get home it will be harder. The more I know you and the more I like you, Hunter, the worse that decision is going to be. Maybe it would be better if I left California and let you and Dad sort this out for yourselves."

"Better for whom?" Hunter asked. "Not for me. I wish I could just say forget it and walk away, but I can't," he said, turning and pulling Ferrin into the shadow of his body. He carefully took her sunglasses from her face and their eyes met.

Her eyes were troubled. He wanted to find a way to relieve her and make her feel that if she gave him access to the past nothing bad would happen to her father. But Hunter had no real idea of what was there. And walking away or letting her walk away from him didn't feel right. He couldn't understand why keeping Ferrin with him was so important. He only knew that it was.

"I would walk away from the past if it would let me go. I would do that for you, honey, but it's out of my hands. Bringing the facts to light is the only thing that will put the past to rest."

Hunter was intense when he stared into her eyes. If the devil looked like Hunter she'd gladly sell her soul to him. But he wasn't asking for her soul. He wasn't even asking for her heart. He was asking for a chance at normal. Something that had always eluded her.

Not because of her father, though there were times when she blamed him for that. But she knew it was all down to her and her ideas of what life and relationships should be. She felt odd a lot of the time because to her it seemed everyone had something normal to draw from. Not her disappointment with her father.

She tipped her head forward and their foreheads touched. She saw that Hunter had closed his eyes, and took advantage of the moment to study his face closely.

She noticed the tiny scar underneath his right eye and how thick his eyelashes were. She brought her hands up to his face, cupped his jaw and felt the feathery smoothness of his beard under her fingers. Hunter captivated her.

She'd been trying to protect herself by throwing up barriers between them. By making her father's files and Hunter's hotness into things that should make her back away. But they didn't. He was complicated and intriguing and he drew her the way a flame drew a moth, even though she was smart and knew she might get burned. She also knew it was worth it.

He was worth it.

And hell, if she were completely honest, she'd admit she was worth it, too. She deserved the chance to be with a man like Hunter. No one said every relationship had to last forever. In fact, she'd be happy with a few weeks. Just something fun.

Surely he could do fun?

He seemed like the poster boy for fun.

She brushed her finger over his soft beard and then his lips. They were firm but also soft. His eyes opened. There was something unreadable in his gaze but she didn't let that bother her. She let the salty sea breeze sweep through her and carry away her worries and her fears. Fear had kept her in that big mansion on the hill in a dark house with a father who by turns resented her and pretended to dote on her. Fear had been responsible for her making those boxes into an ultimatum and fear had driven her out of that house this morning and straight to this man.

Hunter.

"Thank you."

"You're welcome," he said, stepping away. They got back on their boards and returned to the shop and changed. When they both came out of the changing rooms they were awkward. Or maybe it was just her. Hunter came forward and took her hand in his, threading their fingers together again and leading her back toward where they'd left the car. "I can't imagine what it was like growing up with Coach as a father."

"It wasn't bad or good. He just ignored me. I think if I'd been a different sort of person I might have pushed harder to make him notice me. But instead I just stayed in the shadows."

"You weren't always in the shadows, were you?"

"With him I was. I did well in school and my mom and my stepdad are really great. So I had this weird upbringing where I was the center of attention and then I'd come to California for four weeks in the summer and my dad would just leave me be. I think I'm projecting some of that resentment onto you," she admitted. Actually she knew she was doing it. He was one of her father's favorites. It was hard not to want what he had gotten from her dad. Respect. Attention.

"I haven't felt anything like that. It seems more to me that you're afraid to trust yourself. To just let go and be comfortable with me."

"Maybe," she admitted. "But then I don't believe for one second that you are being yourself with me."

He shrugged.

She was starting to notice he did that a lot. Perhaps

he thought it was a nice neutral response. But she saw it as a shield. His way of not answering when a subject cut a little too close to the truth. And she got that. Really she did. She wanted to run away from things that made her feel too much. But running had never worked.

"How about this? You stop shrugging and answer me and I'll try to let go so we can have some fun today."

"I have been having fun. You make me feel again, Ferrin. It's not lust—because that's easy and hormone-driven—but something more. I never thought I'd feel this way around a woman again."

She arched her eyebrow at him. "Am I expected to believe that?"

He gave her a sheepish grin. "Yes, you are. It's true. I want you, I'm not going to deny that, but there is more to it. This isn't a simple conquest."

"I should hope not," she said, but there was lightness in his tone that made her want to smile.

"Which part are you talking about—the simple or the conquest?"

"I guess you'll have to stick around to find out," she said.

"Oh, I intend to," he said.

He put his arms around her and pulled her back against his chest. The sea breeze wrapped around them as they stood facing the horizon and she stopped worrying.

He tipped her chin back against his shoulder and lowered his head to kiss her. His lips moved over hers, taking her mouth slowly—completely.

When they got back on the road, he didn't take her

back to her car but on a drive up the Pacific Coast Highway. They took turns picking songs on the digital radio station and quizzing each other to see who knew the artist singing. They talked about the best food they'd ever eaten—steak in Argentina for him, strawberry shortcake in Plant City, Florida, for her. And for a while she forgot about her father and football and all the things in life that she'd never been able to find peace with.

She forgot that she wasn't sure she could trust Hunter—in fact, somehow in the midst of laughter and confessions about things that seemed small and inconsequential she realized that she had started to trust him. She'd started to show him the real Ferrin Gainer, and unless she was very much mistaken she thought she was seeing Hunter the man, not the NFL player plagued by past scandal.

Five

It had been a little over a week since her day with Hunter. True to his word, he'd left her free to make her decision. It was as if he'd disappeared from her life. She wanted him back. The past week she'd spent a lot of time in this house with Coach. And she still wasn't any closer to a decision.

She stood in the hallway outside his in-home study. The door was solid hardwood and the handle polished brass. It was cold under her hand. Maybe it was her imagination but she sensed her father wouldn't want her in his office.

She opened the door, stepped inside and then quickly closed it behind her.

Ferrin quietly entered the room that she'd avoided since returning to California. She stood there in the doorway remembering when she'd tried to come in here as a teen and her father had simply gestured for her to leave.

A part of her thought maybe that was why she hadn't wanted to let Hunter see the boxes of stuff. She didn't want to be here with someone who belonged. But today there was nothing but an empty room and her father was upstairs in his bed, pretending to sleep so he didn't have to talk to her.

She closed the door behind her and walked over to the large walnut desk that had been a gift from her mother a long time ago. She often wondered how two people so different had fallen in love.

Her mother sometimes said it was infatuation. Just that giddy feeling that happens when two people meet who are so different that they get caught up in the myth of romance and love. Not at all like the solid bond her mother had with Ferrin's stepfather. Dean was a decent guy who was an academic like her mother. They made sense as a couple.

Ferrin pushed aside those thoughts and walked across the hardwood floor. One wall of the room was lined with built-in custom bookcases. Her father was one of the winningest coaches in collegiate football so there were lots of trophies on the shelves. He also had always included pictures of the teams that won. She avoided looking at his glory wall and went instead to his desk.

There was a computer but she knew he seldom used it. She turned it on and started opening the drawers in his desk. Nothing really in them except a stack of letters the housekeeper had put in the top left-hand drawer and a picture of Ferrin underneath them.

It was from her college graduation. She'd had no idea he'd kept it. He hadn't shown up because one of his graduates that year had invited him to go fly-fishing in Montana. It shouldn't have mattered. She'd known for a long time the kind of man her father was.

So why was she working so hard not to upset him? To do what he wanted when he had never done one thing for her?

Because two wrongs didn't make a right.

Her mom's words echoed in her mind. She'd heard them time and again growing up and now they were her constant companion when she wanted to turn away. Wanted to just do what she wanted instead of what was right.

Her father had finally told her that he was against letting Hunter look at the records. She wondered if her father knew something or if he was afraid once he started letting people into his old files they'd officially become the past and Coach wouldn't be relevant anymore. For his part, Hunter had said he'd respect whatever decision she made…but she knew he wouldn't. Had he said that just to make it so she'd say yes?

"Ugh."

The sound of her voice echoed around the glory room her father had made for himself. She went to the walk-in closet where the records had been stored. But then she left the boxes unopened and exited the room altogether. The computer was still on and she didn't care.

She walked through the house that would never be home to her and out the French doors that led to the patio.

The breeze was cool and strong and she stood there, letting her hair whip around her face, hoping it would push away her thoughts and leave just one clear path.

But it didn't.

Nothing was going to happen to force her to make the choice.

She was going to have to decide and then stick to it.

What was her father afraid of?

Workout tapes, practice scrimmages, maybe some celebrations. What was it that her father thought they'd find?

She had to know.

It was one more thing about him that she couldn't put her finger on. Maybe by reading the files and viewing the tapes she'd find answers about the man. Finally be able to understand him.

The decision had to be about her dad, she thought. It couldn't be about Hunter or his questions regarding the past. There was no guarantee that he'd find what he was looking for. In fact, she highly doubted he would. He might never find the answers and the peace he needed.

So it came down to her own decision. What could she live with?

She knew part of it was influenced by her feelings for Hunter, but a bigger part was to figure out what her father had always found in those boys he'd coached that he'd never found in her.

When she came back in from the patio, the house was quiet except for the ticking of the grandfather clock in the hallway. Some of her earliest memories involved that clock. It had been soothing just listening to its solid ticking when her parents had been fighting. She walked over and sank down on the floor in front of it.

The pendulum kept swinging back and forth, the way she swung back and forth between her options for the decision she had to make. One side Coach, the other Hunter.

Coach…ah, that was so complicated.

Hunter…well, it would be nice to just make the man happy and claim some of that happiness for herself.

She heard her ringtone and picked up her phone, glancing at the locked screen. It was a Texas number but not one she recognized.

"Hello?"

"Ferrin, it's Hunter."

His voice was dark and smooth, sending the good kind of shivers down her back. She hadn't wanted to admit it but she'd missed him.

Hunter had gotten up early and driven over to the college. He'd figured that if he found some of the old practice tapes there maybe he wouldn't have to ask Ferrin for them anymore.

But when he arrived, he'd been greeted by former assistant coach Graham Peters coming out of Coach's old office. Peters had been short and blunt—he didn't have any tapes and he thought Hunter should let the whole thing go and leave the past in the past.

As Hunter walked out of the gym and over to his car,

he realized he had no other choice: he was back to need-ing Coach's boxes. It was time to call Ferrin.

Hunter had kept his distance. A part of him hoped she'd call and invite him over to look through Coach's old stuff but she hadn't. And he'd waited a week.

The past seven or eight days had felt too long. He was used to action. Even though he knew he was mov-ing only ten yards at a time toward the end zone, he still wanted some forward momentum.

He'd been busy with his charity. Working with Gabi, Hunter was going to sponsor the local peewee football league at the children's recreation center she'd helped Kingsley get permission to build. And there was a cer-tain amount of work he could do to keep his days busy and his mind off Ferrin, but the nights…damn if he didn't spend every night wishing he'd done more than kiss her on the beach.

He was trying to be the good guy. But it was hard.

He had made a few calls to the people they had in common. Coach's old secretary at the college had given him Ferrin's cell phone number when he explained that he had visited with Coach and didn't want to disturb him by calling the house. Coach's old secretary had al-ways had a soft spot for Hunter back in his playing days.

Though he knew it would be better if she called him, he dialed the number and waited.

Her voice on the phone was sweet and he could pic-ture the smile on her face as she spoke. He missed her.

How? He'd known her a week but he missed her.

He needed to get himself in check. He blamed King-sley and Gabi and how they made him want to think about his own future in a way he hadn't before. It was different with Kingsley's first wife, who'd been a supermodel and had her own life. They hadn't been much of a family.

Until he'd seen Gabi, Conner and Kingsley together, Hunter hadn't realized that he wanted one for himself.

Ferrin broke into his thoughts. "Hunter. I was wondering if you'd given up and gone back to...where do you normally live?"

"Well, you know I own a house here," he said. "But I had been based in Malibu prior to moving up here."

"Oh, why did you move?"

"To be closer to my godson."

"Conner, right?"

"Yes."

He heard a heavy sigh. "I'm afraid I still haven't made a decision about the boxes."

Dammit.

"Okay. I was calling to invite you to dinner with my friends."

"You were?"

"Yes. No pressure," he said.

"Um...which friends?"

"Conner and his parents," Hunter said.

"When?"

"Tonight. Just casual. I think it's taco night," Hunter said.

"Taco night?"

"Gabi does themed dinner nights," Hunter said.

"That sounds so cute. Okay, I will go with you. What time?" Ferrin asked.

Hunter looked at the iMessage he'd just sent to Kingsley asking for the time and saw he'd responded.

"Seven. I could pick you up at six thirty," Hunter said.

"Sounds good. What can I bring?"

"Just bring yourself. Hang on while I text Kingsley."

He typed a quick message back to Kingsley confirming they'd both be at his place for dinner.

Kingsley texted back with a smiley face emoji.

"What have you been doing?" Ferrin asked when they resumed the conversation. "More of your charity work?"

Hunter leaned back in his office chair, crossing his feet at the ankles.

"Yes. Just finalizing the equipment for the peewee league here in Carmel. Kingsley donated the money for a new community recreation center and now my charity is providing the stuff they need to get playing."

He heard her moving around and wondered what she was doing. Had he interrupted something important?

"What have you been up to?"

"Trying to make Coach eat all his meals and convince him to sit outside part of every day."

She'd brought up Coach…maybe he'd just mention the tapes. That was what he was truly interested in. The information that Daria Miller, a reporter who'd gone to school with Hunter, King and Gabi, had uncovered involved women being drugged and raped, possibly by other players on the team that year. But was it only rumor? So far no one would come forward and talk to him or Kingsley. Was he chasing after another false lead?

"I bet that's not easy." He wasn't going to pressure her, no matter how much that went against his instincts. He knew that the only way he was ever going to see what was in the files was if Ferrin or Coach decided to let him.

"He's very stubborn. Maybe you have some tips you can give me," she said.

"Why would I?" he asked.

She made a noise that he couldn't interpret over the phone.

"He always related better to the guys on his team than to me. I wondered if there was some wisdom you might have that I'm missing," Ferrin said.

That broken relationship with her father again. Hunter wanted to fix it for her, but he wasn't exactly Dr. Phil. He was more Steve Wilkos: full-on confrontation.

"Tell him that every day, every small improvement is going to show up on game day. Remind him that for him every day is game day. He needs to keep working until he reaches the end zone and can get out of bed and back to his old life."

"Football analogies?"

"It's what he loves."

"Is it what you love?" she countered.

"It used to be," he said.

"When did it stop being?"

"When I put the game in front of a person I cared for and I lost her," Hunter admitted. Part of the reason he had to resolve what had happened to Stacia was the guilt that no amount of time could dull. He still carried it with him.

"I'm sorry."

"Thanks. But it was my own fault. I think Coach needs a wake-up call. He's a good man," Hunter said. Coach had always defended him and Kingsley, and Hunter would never forget that. Even his brothers and his parents had a few questions before they were convinced he was innocent. Only Coach had always known it.

"I'll try. But he doesn't…he doesn't seem to want to get out of bed at all. Do you think you could talk to some of your teammates and maybe that would help motivate him?" Ferrin said.

"I'll see what I can do," he said, his heart sinking that he wasn't any closer to getting access to Coach's records as the call came to an end.

After hanging up with Hunter, Ferrin heard the house phone ring and waited to see if Joy was going to answer it. It was odd to get a call on that line and she suspected it might be someone from the college for her dad.

"Hello."

"Hello. This is Graham Peters. May I speak to Coach Gainer?"

"I'm sorry, he's not available right now. May I have him call you back?"

"No, you may not. I was his assistant coach at the college. Who is this?" the man asked. His voice was brusque and he was impatient.

"Ferrin, Coach's daughter."

"Coach has a daughter. I didn't know that," Graham said. "I was very sorry to hear about your dad's strokes and heart attack. How is he doing?"

He sounded much nicer now that he knew she was Coach's daughter and not the housekeeper. Ferrin wondered how often Joy had to put up with that kind of treatment. Graham's name didn't mean anything to her but she quickly Googled it and his photo and a bio from the college website popped up.

"He's recovering but it's slow. What did you need to speak to him about?" Ferrin asked.

"We would like to honor your father with a tribute at the college. I was hoping to come over and go through his old practice tapes to put together a montage of his best moments," Graham said. "I was calling to see when I could come over."

"I don't think he's up for visitors. I'm happy to look through his boxes, though," she said.

"I don't want you to have to do that. Maybe I'll call back next week and see if he's any better."

"Okay," Ferrin said. "That would be fine. I'll let him know you called, Graham."

"Thanks," he said, hanging up the phone. She wondered what was in those boxes that everyone wanted to look at and her father wasn't interested in sharing. She suspected that for her father, it would be bittersweet for him to be reminded of a time when he was young and fit and healthy.

A little while later, when it was almost lunchtime, Ferrin went into the kitchen.

"I'll take his lunch tray up," Ferrin said to Joy. Then

she remembered how reluctant he was to leave his room. "On second thought, would you mind setting up our lunch on the patio by the pool? I think it will be nice to get him outside."

"I don't mind setting it up out there, but how are you going to convince him to come downstairs?" Joy asked.

"Leave that to me," Ferrin said. Armed with her new advice from Hunter, she was pretty sure she could motivate him to get out of the bed.

She climbed the stairs and realized the song "Walking on Sunshine" was running through her mind. Really? One call from Hunter and now she was energized.

She paused midway up and stood there. She knew the psychology of falling for someone. Understood that the newness of it could flood the body with euphoria. But she'd never experienced it herself before. She didn't want to fall for a man. Especially one like Hunter, who was clearly not going to be long in her life. It was complicated. It made no sense.

But she couldn't deny that for the first time in a week she felt peppy.

She hurried up the steps and knocked on her dad's door.

"Come in."

She opened the door and stepped inside. The room was dark, gloomy. The curtains were closed. She walked over and opened them as she had when she'd come up for breakfast.

"Who closed these?"

"I did. The sun is so bright today," he said.

"I'm glad to hear you got up to close them," Ferrin

said, ignoring his grumpiness. "We are having lunch downstairs."

"What?"

"Doctor's orders, I'm afraid." A little white lie never hurt anything, she thought. She just needed him out of this room. Maybe he'd find something to renew his happiness.

"Told you she had it in for me. She knows I can't get out of the bed," he said.

"By your own words you closed the drapes."

"Damn, heard that, did ya?"

She smiled at him. There were moments when he was the father she'd always wanted. "Yup. Now up and at 'em."

"I'm not sure I can," he said.

"Really?" she asked, walking over to the bed. "You told me that you don't want to retire, but you will have no choice unless you get up. The thing is, you aren't going to be able to do it all at once. Just one small step each day."

"You think?"

"I know. Isn't that what you would tell your players?"

"Touché."

Pushing the covers back, he swung his pajama-covered legs over the side. He was a big man, almost six-four, and he was solid. She came to his side and offered him her arm, which he took to stand up. He held on to her as he carefully rose. Their eyes met and for the first time in her life she felt as though her father needed her.

Being here while he lay in bed hadn't really made

her feel like anything other than a glorified nursemaid. But this…this mattered.

He shuffled over to his chair and she helped him sit down so he could put his slippers on.

"I'm pretty weak," he admitted.

"You are. That's why we are having lunch outside."

She helped him stand up again and he took a few steps on his own and then walked toward the door. It was as if he was trying to make sure he knew his own limitations.

"I've always made my guys who were recovering from an injury get back on the field. Made them move. I guess I needed someone to make me do it."

"Guess so," Ferrin said.

"Thanks, sunshine," he said, before opening the door and making his way carefully down the stairs.

Ferrin followed him down the stairs, wondering how much of their problems was down to her always falling back on childhood disappointments. Maybe she and her dad should start with a clean slate. Start over so she could get to know him as an adult.

Joy was waiting at the bottom of the stairs, watching their slow progress. She winked at Ferrin as Coach stepped off the stairs and made his way out to the patio.

"Good job," Joy said.

"He was ready," Ferrin admitted. But she was secretly pleased.

She stopped in the kitchen to don a beach hat and her sunglasses before picking up her father's college baseball cap and his sunglasses.

She handed them to him as she joined him at the

table. Coach stared out at the horizon and she wondered what he saw out there.

"What are you looking at?" she asked.

"Your mom and I used to talk about buying a boat," he said suddenly.

Ferrin figured it wouldn't help him to know that her mom and stepdad had one that they took out on the lake every weekend. "Why didn't you?"

"I was busy and you were little. Didn't want you to drown. You weren't very strong as a kid."

"Strong? I was healthy," Ferrin said.

"Yeah, but you weren't outdoorsy," he said. "I tried to teach you to swim but you cried. I tried to teach you to play football, again with the crying."

"I'm sensing a theme here," she said. "I remember you tossing me into the pool."

"Yeah, your instincts never really kicked in," he said.

"That's not how you teach a kid to swim," she said.

"It's how my dad did it," he said to her. He looked at her and not for the first time she realized how little she knew about her father.

"I never knew that. What was he like?"

"Like? He was a man. He told me to do something and expected me to do it. I think he was proud that I played ball and when I got the coaching job...he liked always coming to the games," Coach said.

"I wish I'd met him," Ferrin said.

"No use wishing for things that can't be."

And that sort of reminded her that he hadn't really changed.

"What the hell is this?" he asked, looking down at his plate. "I told Joy I wasn't eating any more salads."

"The doctor insists. You know you had a heart attack," she said.

"Don't sass me, Ferrin. I'm aware of my health issues," he said.

She folded her hands together on the table. "One of your players told me to remind you that games are won by showing up every day and making small improvements. You can't beat this if you stay in bed and eat junk."

"Good advice," he said. "Which player of mine told you that?"

"Hunter. Hunter Caruthers," she said. Of course, he'd take Hunter's advice but not hers or the doctor's.

"Hunter?"

"Yes. Do you remember he came to visit you?"

He nodded. "I'm not feeling so well. Get Joy to bring this rabbit food up to my room."

Ferrin got to her feet, worried about him. But he shrugged her off.

"I'm fine, girl. I can get back upstairs."

Hurt, she sat back down. "I'm not going to be here for dinner. I have plans."

"Fine. See you tomorrow then."

He shuffled away and she sat there watching him. Why did she keep trying to break through to him? When was enough going to be enough?

Six

Kingsley Buchanan's house was nice. Okay, it was gorgeous. His fiancée was a whip-smart Latina with beautiful skin and hair and a laugh that was infectious. Conner was adorable. But what really captured Ferrin's attention was the way that Hunter was with the toddler.

Hunter's guard was down.

She'd tried to see the man behind the charm and when he was with Conner she was pretty sure she saw that man. He was open, and the affection he felt for his godson was clearly visible on his face.

"Ready for some football?" Conner asked. "Daddy taught me to throw."

Given that Kingsley had been a very big deal quarterback in the NFL based on the trophies and pictures she'd seen as they'd walked through the house earlier, Ferrin was betting on Conner being very good at throwing.

"I am, buddy," Hunter said. "But Ferrin can't catch. Can you help me teach her?"

She groaned.

"Really?" Conner asked. "Ever'body can catch."

"Not me," she admitted.

Conner came over to her. The football was too big and he held it with both hands against his body. He tipped his head back to stare up at her. "Unca Hunter can teach you. He showed me and I'm good."

"I bet you are the best."

He smiled up at her and she felt her heart melt a little. Being a mom wasn't something that she'd ever really had on her radar. She knew that just having a kid wasn't a guarantee that a person would be a good parent and she wasn't sure how the genetics would work out for her. Would she be like her mom or her dad?

Why chance it?

But seeing this sweet little boy, his smile and his earnest way of speaking, made her think about it.

"It's easy," Conner said. He held the football with one arm and then reached for her hand and drew her down the hall.

Hunter watched her with amusement in his eyes and something else she couldn't really define as he followed them out to the yard.

"Stand here," Conner said.

He positioned her in the yard where he wanted her and walked back over to Hunter, who had followed them out. Conner handed the ball to Hunter and looked up at his godfather for a long minute.

"You're better at catching than throwing," he said.

"I am. But I still throw farther than you," Hunter said.

"Not for long," Kingsley said as he joined them, scooping his son up and propping him on his shoulder. "Conner's got my arm."

"You think he should throw the ball to Ferrin?" Hunter asked. "She's never caught a ball."

Something passed between the two men and Ferrin started to worry that they might see her as a charity case. Why had she told him she couldn't catch? She'd managed fairly well in her daily life without catching all this time.

"Maybe," Kingsley said. "Why don't you coach her on catching while I give this monkey some advice."

King turned Conner upside down and the little boy dropped the ball as he started laughing. Safe in his father's arms, he wasn't afraid of falling or of failing. She felt a pang because she'd never experienced that.

Grow up, she thought.

She smiled at the laughter that filled the backyard and shook off her feelings. Her father wasn't this kind of hands-on dad and she had to admit that she loved the fact that Kingsley was.

Hunter came around behind her. He didn't touch her but she felt the heat from his body all along her back. She remembered the way he'd felt at the beach when he'd kissed her.

She shivered and he put one hand on her shoulder.

She glanced back at him. The intensity in his eyes suggested he remembered their kiss, too.

"Okay, so catching…"

"Yes, catching," she said. He put his hands on her shoulders, his touch moving slowly down her arms to her hands, which he cupped in his. "You're creating a pocket for the ball. You aren't catching it so much as giving it a safe place to land. Once you feel the tip of the ball in the pocket then close your hands. The grip is going to be awkward but that's okay. Once you have the nose in your hands, you've got it. And no one is going to tackle you."

"That's a huge relief," she said. Her hands shook a little bit and she realized she wanted to be good at this. That she wanted to be able to catch this ball. What if she didn't? Would Hunter get disgusted and walk away? Or lose his temper? Not that she'd seen any evidence of that.

"Good. Now, in the past when you've caught the ball, what was the hardest part?" he asked.

"Keeping my eyes open. It's unnerving to see something hurtling at me," she admitted.

"Fair enough. I'm going to let you in on a secret," he said.

She turned to face him because being in his arms made it really hard to concentrate and she wanted to hear his secrets.

"Yes?"

"I don't always look either. I run a pattern and then I get to the spot where I'm supposed to be. The rest of it is up to King. He has to hit the target."

She tossed her head back and laughed. "Target? That right there is why catching sounds scary."

"He won't throw it that hard. Do you want me to help the first time?" he asked, putting his hands on her shoulders and turning her to face Conner and Kingsley, who were both waiting.

"No," she said, taking a deep breath. "I have to do this on my own."

Plus it was distracting to have him pressed against her.

"Okay."

Hunter took a few steps away from her. She watched him moving with that smooth fluid grace that always took her breath away. Then he stopped and gave Kingsley a hard look.

Kingsley smiled and nodded and she realized that she was being set up to succeed. For the first time in her life a man—an athlete—was determined that she would be good at something associated with football. She didn't bother to analyze the warmth that started in her stomach and spread throughout her body. She knew it was affection.

She'd just never guessed it would feel so good.

She cupped her hands the way that Hunter had showed her and Kingsley handed the ball to Conner, who drew his arm back and let the ball fly with more power than she'd expected. She immediately understood he'd been training with his father for a while.

It was all she could do to keep one eye open as the ball headed toward her. But she did it. She took a step forward to catch the ball and it landed in her hands with a solid thump. She hesitated for a moment and then closed her hands around it.

"I caught the ball!"

Hunter let out a whoop and Kingsley and Conner applauded as she opened her hands and let the ball fall to the ground. Hunter scooped her up in his arms and twirled her around.

"I couldn't have done it any better," he said, bringing his mouth down on hers.

Watching Ferrin catch the ball that Conner had thrown was fun. *Fun.*

It wasn't a word that he routinely applied to his life. How could he?

Before he retired from playing he'd been busy working out and taking hits. He'd stayed out of the locker room after games to avoid the press, and aside from showing up on TMZ and in gossip magazines very occasionally, he'd done a good job of keeping his private life private.

"Hunter?" Kingsley called his name.

"Hmm?"

"I asked if you were going to San Francisco tomorrow for the opening of the latest Seconds nightclub," Kingsley said.

"Sounds very exciting," Ferrin said. "I don't think I've been to a nightclub since I graduated college."

"It should be a lot of fun. Conner is going to stay with a nanny from Gabi's agency while we go out," Kingsley said.

"Normally my parents would watch him," Gabi said. "But they are going, too."

"To a nightclub?" Ferrin asked.

Hunter smiled. "Gabi's cousin is a co-owner. Guillermo de la Cruz."

"I didn't make the connection," Ferrin said. "So you are related to the Spanish aristocracy?"

"Very distant. I'm in the branch that left that all behind," Gabi said with a smile.

"Gonna see my new cousins," Conner said.

"Now that we are engaged, Conner is calling Gui's girls his cousins. In fact, you should be heading to bed, young man," Kingsley said. "We are leaving early."

"Okay. But I need a bath and bedtime story," Conner said.

"You two should take a walk in the gardens. We will be back soon," Gabi said.

Gabi and Kingsley got up and took Conner with them as they left the dining room. Hunter looked over at Ferrin; she was toying with the stem of her wineglass, spinning it between her fingers.

"So, do you like my friends?"

"I do. They're very nice. I am definitely seeing a different man here than I did at the beach and at Coach's house."

"Good. I want you to know me better," he said.

"Well, this is very nice. Not like the other night at dinner when it was like being in a fishbowl. I guess you are used to your celebrity," she said.

"Not really," he admitted. But it wasn't celebrity

drawing their attention but notoriety that had been the cause of the stares. "Want to walk in the garden?"

"Yes," she said, pushing her chair back and getting to her feet. He led the way out of the house to the manicured gardens. There was landscape lighting to lead their way through the shrubs and plants. In the center of the garden was a stone patio with a fire pit that someone had laid earlier. The night was comfortable so he led the way to one of the benches and gestured for Ferrin to sit down.

He should ask her again about the files. Try to get what he needed from her. But he didn't want to pressure her. He liked Ferrin and wanted...a future?

Right. He had no future unless he could clear up the mystery of Stacia's death. And his gut was saying the answer was on those missing gym tapes.

She tipped her head back and glanced up at the sky. It was hard to see the stars here, but the moon was full. Big and bright. She nibbled her bottom lip and he wondered what was going on in her mind.

She wasn't carrying around the past like a fifty-pound weight the way he was. "What's on your mind?"

Wrapping her arm around her waist, she looked over at him, but her eyes didn't meet his. "I was jealous of a toddler today."

"Conner has a great life," Hunter said. "I think he deserves it but I can see why it might inspire jealousy."

"No you can't. Even though you wanted to be a football player instead of a cowboy, you still had something to connect with your dad."

"You didn't?"

"No. Part of the reason I'm reluctant to go through any of Dad's files is the fact that it stirs up old resentments. Old feelings of inadequacy in myself."

He draped his arm over her shoulder and hugged her. "But you can catch now."

She laughed but it was forced.

"What's the matter?"

"Not everything can be laughed away. I'm twenty-five, Hunter. I shouldn't be jealous of a toddler because his dad loves him," she said. "Maybe that's too intense for you and not what you are thinking about in terms of me and you, but there it is. Those files you want to look at, I'd just as soon burn them, because they represent everything that he loved more than me."

Hunter let his arm fall from her shoulders and leaned forward, putting his head in his hands. God, he didn't need these complications—he needed to see those files. He'd gone as far as he could with stories and hearsay. He needed some kind of evidence that other co-eds had been attacked so that the girls involved could come forward and help them find the person who'd killed Stacia. He sympathized with how Ferrin was struggling with her past. Being back in the house that was Coach's and not really hers was making her a little edgy. Hunter understood. But how would he ever get past barriers like this?

"I joke because it pisses me off, Ferrin. It makes me mad on your behalf. You're right when you said my dad and I connected. He might have thought I was being foolish to try to make a living off of football but he loved me enough to give me the room to try. I don't understand how Coach could be so good at motivating us and so horrible at parenting you.

"And I'm frustrated that no matter how much I show you my life and myself you keep doubting me. I get that you don't want to upset your dad—believe I understand it more than you probably think I do—but I need those answers to be able to see a future for myself. I want those files to make sure that when Conner goes to school kids don't point and stare because their parents remember King and I being arrested for a murder we didn't commit. And I want Stacia to finally rest in peace."

"I'm sorry," she said, quietly. "Truly I am. It might seem selfish to you—"

"It doesn't. I meant it when I said I get how delicate your relationship with your father is."

"Maybe—"

"Don't. I don't want you to make a promise that will be hard to keep. Just know that nothing with you is a game to me."

He couldn't push her further for access to the records. Not now. He wanted Ferrin to feel comfortable with him and in her own skin. He sat back and she put her head on his shoulder.

Ferrin pulled away as they heard footsteps behind them.

"Sorry to interrupt but Ferrin's phone keeps ringing," Kingsley said.

She sprang to her feet as if she'd been given a reprieve and he wondered if that was how she felt. After all, she kept blowing hot and cold with him. Hunter didn't let it bother him. He was playing a game. A long game. Games weren't won by Hail Mary passes.

Kingsley sat down next to him on the bench.

"I was going to ask if you'd had a chance to talk her into letting you see Coach's files but I can see that you weren't thinking about the past," King said.

"I wasn't," Hunter admitted. "I'm playing the long game."

"Don't get hurt," King warned. "She's not the only one who can fall for it."

"I'm not playing with her, not like that, Kingsley. It's just I want her to want me to see the files. If I bribe or force or seduce her into it…she'll always remember that about me."

Kingsley clapped him on the shoulder.

"I wish we could go back ten years and keep our younger selves from—"

"Don't say it. I wish that, too. But we both know we can't. You've managed to make a new start for yourself. There's nothing wrong with that. I'm going to figure it out, too. You know it takes me twice as long as you to do anything."

Kingsley laughed the way that Hunter wanted him to. He wouldn't think about going back in time because he wasn't sure he'd even do things differently. Not breaking up with Stacia would have meant spending a life together that he knew both of them would regret.

But at least she'd be alive.

Yeah, there was that.

His father had once said there were no such things as shortcuts and finally Hunter felt as if he got it. He'd been paying for every mistake he'd made and everything he wanted. The price didn't bother him most days, but on nights like this one when he wanted to be an average guy on a date with a pretty woman, it did.

He needed something from her. But if he wasn't careful he'd end up hurting her.

"Are you going to bring her to San Francisco for the Seconds party?" Kingsley asked.

"I want to. I don't know if she can be away from her father for that long so I'll have to check," Hunter said.

"Good. I think the more she gets to know us the more inclined she'll be to let you see Coach's files."

"I hope so," Hunter said.

"If you think it would be easier, I don't mind playing the heavy. I'm actually really good about getting what I want," Kingsley said.

Hunter didn't like the idea of Kingsley manipulating Ferrin any more than he liked the thought of doing it himself.

"Ten yards at a time," Hunter said.

Kingsley laughed. "Just like Coach always said."

"It's as true off the field as on. I mean it's the only way I have been able to stay positive and think that one day we will find the answers."

"You know something?" Kingsley said, getting to his feet. "Me, too. Let's go find the ladies and have a drink. Then you can ask Ferrin to go with us to San Fran. I'll be there for moral support."

More like to mock him if he made a mess of the asking. "Whatever. I don't need a wing man with Ferrin."

"Are you sure?"

"Yeah, I am."

Kingsley led the way back to the house, where Gabi and Ferrin were sitting in the kitchen, each sipping a glass of wine.

"Everything okay?" Hunter asked her, sitting down.

"Yes. It was just my mom," she said, blushing. "I hadn't called her in a few days so she wanted to check on me."

"Moms are like that," Gabi said. "Mine stops by the house if I don't call her every day."

"Made for a few uncomfortable moments," Kingsley said.

Everyone laughed. Hunter was looking down at the table when he felt Ferrin's fingers on the back of his hand. "Do you mind taking me home? I know it's early but I want to check in on Coach."

"No problem."

They said goodbye to Gabi and Kingsley and Hunter took the circuitous route home. The night sky was clear and the full moon lit the way.

"Thank you for helping me catch that football tonight," she said.

"You did all the work. I just offered a few tips."

"Well, the tips worked. Listen, football is my Achilles' heel and tonight you made me almost like it. That means more than you could know," she said. "Also thank you for not pressuring me about Coach's files and stuff. That makes it a lot easier to just relax and get to know you."

"Is it working?" he asked. But he knew he'd sort of pressured her by telling her what those files meant to him.

"Yes," she said with that sweet, innocent smile.

"Would you like to come to San Francisco with me for the party at Seconds?" he asked.

"I'd love to."

"I'm not sure if you can be away from your dad overnight but we can stay with some friends of mine or we can drive back after the party."

"I'll let you know after I talk to Joy. If she can stay the night with Dad then I should be fine," Ferrin said.

Seven

"Good morning, Joy," Ferrin said as she came into the kitchen.

Joy jumped and then turned down the volume on the TV she'd been watching. "Just getting my morning fix of gossip."

"Anything good?" Ferrin asked as she poured herself a cup of coffee.

"Not really. I was hoping to see something about one of my boys," she said.

Joy was a huge fan of boy bands and hadn't stopped hoping that One Direction would get back together. She thought they were sweet young men who just needed some time to straighten themselves out.

"I'll take Coach's tray up to him while you keep watching," she said.

"Thanks, Ferrin. Oh, a man named Graham called for you yesterday. Said he'd try back today," Joy said.

Graham Peters. She didn't really want to talk to him again. "He asked to come and go through Dad's stuff. I told him no. Dad gets really agitated when anyone from the college is mentioned. Have you noticed?"

"I have," Joy said. "I think he's still upset they 'retired' him instead of letting him come back to work."

"I agree. Let's just keep putting Graham off until I talk to Coach."

"I will."

"Are you sure you'll be okay watching Coach overnight?" Ferrin asked before leaving. Joy had agreed to stay the night but Ferrin wanted to make sure the other woman didn't feel pressured to do so.

"I don't mind."

Good. Now all she had to do was make sure her father would be okay if she left. And maybe try to figure out what to do about Coach's files that everyone seemed to want to get their hands on.

The house on Beacon Hill that Hunter took her to was a restored Victorian that looked like a picture postcard from the past. The Tiffany stained glass windows and painted wood trims all added to the ambiance. She was nervous.

Why wouldn't she be?

She'd never gone away for a night with a man before. The men she dated tended to be like her. Homebodies who were happy to spend date night sitting in front of the television with a tub of popcorn watching movies.

They had taken a limo down to San Francisco. They'd left the sunroof open, and she'd pretended to be glamorous. But her thick, curly hair had whipped around her head until she'd finally given up and pulled it back into a messy bun. She had her sunglasses on and was dressed casually as was Hunter. She wore a pair of cigarette pants that ended at the ankle, a red-striped top and a pair of ballet flats.

When the door to the home opened and she glanced up at the woman standing there, Ferrin felt unkempt by comparison. The other woman had straight hair that hung neatly to her shoulders, and she wore a chic sundress. She waved at Hunter and smiled over at Ferrin.

"I'm so glad you are here," she said. Her accent was American but had a patrician sound to it.

"We are, too," Hunter said. "Ferrin, come and meet Kara, Gui's wife. She and I are distant cousins through our fathers."

"That's right, a long time ago, we were into oil," she said. "But that was a really long time ago. Now I'm into kids." Three little girls poked their heads around her legs. The eldest couldn't have been more than five. They were adorable with their thick black hair—two of them with curls and the youngest with straight hair like her mother.

"Hello, cherubs," Hunter said, dropping down on one knee as the girls came running toward him. They all jumped on him and he hugged them close before he stood up.

The eldest came over to Ferrin and tipped her head

back. The little girl had big brown eyes with the thickest eyelashes that Ferrin had ever seen. "I'm Zara."

Ferrin stooped down so she was on eye level with the little girl. "Ferrin. Very nice to meet you."

"Nice to meet you, too," she said. "We are making cookies. Do you want to help?"

"I'd love to," Ferrin said.

"You don't have to," Kara piped up. "It's a messy endeavor."

"I don't mind at all," Ferrin said. Zara slipped her hand into Ferrin's and led the way inside the house. Hunter followed close on her heels.

"This is Chloe and that's Luisa," Zara said as they walked past her sisters.

"You smell pretty," Chloe said.

"I like your hair," Luisa said.

The little girls all crowded around her as they entered the kitchen, talking a mile a minute. When she sat down at the kitchen table—as directed by Zara—Luisa climbed on Ferrin's lap and touched one of her curls. She was the youngest daughter with the straight brown hair.

Ferrin wondered if Luisa wished she looked more like her sisters. "What do you want to be when you grow up?"

"A princess knight," Luisa said without even hesitating.

"That's silly, Lu," Zara said.

"Papa said I could be. Mama!" Luisa jumped down from Ferrin's lap and dashed into the hallway where Kara and Hunter were talking.

"She's such a baby," Zara said with the attitude that could only come from being the eldest child. "Chloe, show Ferrin how to stir the cookies."

Chloe came over and climbed up on the chair next to Ferrin. "We just have to add the chocolate chips. Mama keeps them up on that shelf."

Chloe pointed to the location and Ferrin stood up to get them. She brought the bag back over as Hunter entered. "Suckered Ferrin into getting you some chocolates, I see."

"They are for the cookies," Ferrin said. "Are you allergic?" she asked Chloe.

"No, she's not. She's just a chocolate fiend," Hunter explained.

"Papa is, too," Chloe said with a smile that was two parts angel, one part devil. "I wasn't going to eat them," Chloe said as she snuck one into her mouth.

Ferrin hid her smile as she poured a handful of chocolate morsels into the dough and let a few miss the bowl and land in front of Chloe. Hunter grabbed one and then scooped Chloe up and settled her next to him on the bench she'd been kneeling on. He reached for the bag of chocolate and poured a handful for Chloe and himself.

"Better hurry up with that stirring, Ferrin, or they might just be butter cookies."

Ferrin noticed that Hunter was a natural with kids. First with Conner and now Kara's girls. Why hadn't he found a woman to settle down with? She knew that he had the controversy of the Frat House Murder in his past, but that was ten years ago, and he'd been declared innocent. She knew he worried about other kids' reactions to Conner at school. Was that what held him back? Plus, NFL players had no shortage of women who wanted to be with them. Why not Hunter?

"You're staring not stirring, woman," Hunter said.

"Yeah, woman," Chloe added with a laugh.

"Chloe Angelina, are you into my secret stash?" Kara asked as she entered the kitchen with Luisa by her side.

"Yes, but I needed them for my cookies," Chloe said. "And Uncle Hunter wanted them."

"Uncle Hunter is a bad influence," Kara said with a wink at Hunter. "How are the cookies coming?"

"Well, I incorporated as many chocolate chips as I could," Ferrin said.

Kara came over and looked down into the bowl. "Looks good. I say we let Uncle Hunter and the girls put them on the tray and in the oven while we get to know each other."

"Can he do that?"

"Woman—"

"Enough of calling me woman," Ferrin said.

"Fair enough, but I'm a world-class cookie maker. Isn't that right, girls?"

The children all had huge grins on their faces as they nodded and smiled over at her and Kara. She knew they were up to something but it wasn't until Kara led her out into the hall and put her finger over her lips, pointing for her to look back inside, that she figured out what it was.

Hunter and the girls were all eating the dough out of the bowl with a spoon.

"Do they always do this?" Ferrin asked.

"Yes. They love it when he visits."

"Is it dangerous to eat the dough?"

"Not in the small amount he allows. But they feel like they are sneaking around with him and they like it."

"Don't all girls?" Ferrin asked.

Kara laughed. "Yes."

Gui, Tristan and Christos had formed Seconds night-club because they were rich boys without a shot at running their families' companies. Over the years they had all settled down and married. Christos's brother had died and Christos had taken over the running of his family's shipping line. Tristan was second in command at the largest magazine publisher in the world. And Gui, well, Gui sort of took care of the day-to-day management of Seconds and his family. He wasn't interested in the corporate world.

As soon as Kingsley had arrived with Gabi and Conner, the women had dashed out for an impromptu shopping trip and the men were now happily sitting in the living room watching the kids.

Hunter wanted this for himself. He knew that his chances of having a wife and kids were diminished by the past. Not because there was a chance he'd be charged again in Stacia's murder but because it was unresolved in his mind and in the minds of many others who'd followed the case.

"Dude, you look way too serious for *Peppa Pig*," Kingsley said.

Suddenly these cute kids and happy men were too much for him. "I know. I need some air."

He got up and let himself out of the house, walking down Beacon Hill toward the water.

"Hunter, wait," Kingsley called. "I need some air, too."

Kingsley caught up with him and the two men walked in silence for a while.

"Talk to me," Kingsley said. "I am trying to read the play but nothing makes sense. We are closer than ever to getting some real answers about Stacia, you have a great woman in your life and it seems like we are finally making up for the mistakes we made in college. Help me understand what's going on with you."

Hunter stopped and looked out over the bay. It was chilly here but the cold didn't really bother him. In fact it suited the mood he was in today.

"We're not close."

"Why not?" King asked.

Hunter looked down at his feet and pushed his sunglasses up on his head as he looked over at Kingsley. "I can't go through with seducing Ferrin into letting me look in Coach's files anymore. It's not right. I have to let her decide on her own. Her dad doesn't want me looking in his records, and she still doesn't want to go behind Coach's back. It's bringing up a lot of stuff from her childhood—he wasn't a very good father and the existence of these files is painful to her in a way. I almost think I need to back off."

"That sucks," Kingsley said. "Want me to ask her?"

"No. I think that will simply make things worse." Hunter stopped, turned to look at King and felt that brotherly love between them. He shook his head. "I don't think that will help at all. I know I have to do this. I'm going to do it. But I just… I keep getting caught up in this life that I never really thought I'd have."

"I know what you mean."

"How could you? You have Conner and now Gabi. You seem to be better at moving on that I am."

"Well, not really. I always closed myself off before Gabi. And you have a lot more guilt than I do. You have to forgive yourself for not being able to save Stacia, Hunter. You've never been able to do that."

"How can I forgive myself when I still don't know what happened?" It was a question he'd asked himself more than once and the answer still evaded him. "The things I do remember from that night don't make me like myself at all. I was spoiled when I broke up with her. Afraid that if I had a girlfriend I might not be able to enjoy all the perks of being a professional football player."

"If Stacia hadn't died, would you feel the same?" King asked.

Hunter rubbed the back of his neck and put his head down. "I don't know. It doesn't matter anyway, she is dead. And we were both too drunk to remember seeing anything that night. There's no chance for someone like Ferrin and me until I figure this out. No chance."

"She likes you, Hunter. Not because of the football or your money or because you're dangerous. Somehow she likes you."

"Don't take this the wrong way but you're not exactly intuitive," Hunter said.

"You're right, I'm not. But Gabi is. She's convinced Ferrin's the one who will help you move on."

Gabi was convinced. If only it would be that easy to convince Ferrin, but he knew it wouldn't be. "Do you think Coach is protecting someone?"

Better to talk about the past, which he knew and was comfortable with, than the future and Ferrin, which made him feel out of control.

"It's the only thing that makes sense to me," Kingsley said. "You said he recognized you."

"Yeah, but then he got sort of vague. From what Ferrin said he has pieces of memories but not the entire picture."

"So either he's protecting someone because he remembered or he's not sure what's going on and is afraid," Kingsley said. "I wish we'd been able to talk to him before he had the stroke."

"Me, too," Hunter said. But a part of him was glad they hadn't. Ferrin wouldn't have been at Coach's before his health failed and he'd have never met her.

Calmness spread through him as he realized that no matter what happened he wouldn't trade these few weeks with Ferrin for anything. That scared him like nothing else had. Ferrin mattered to him and he knew he was destined to let her down.

Ferrin had enjoyed the afternoon shopping with the women. She had some good girlfriends back in Texas and she realized how much she missed them. She needed to make plans to leave her father and go back home. She knew she was staying now for Hunter. Sure, he wanted permission from her to go through her dad's old files, and if she were honest she'd have to admit she was leaning toward giving it to him.

But she'd wanted more time to get to know him. A part of her was afraid if she just let him have access to her father's files he'd find what he needed and then…leave. That was what she'd been afraid to admit to herself. It didn't take a genius to realize that Hunter wasn't exactly the boy next door. He was very focused on her, very interested, and she was so scared to believe it might be for herself and not for the files. So she was stalling so she wouldn't have to find out.

Coward.

"Are you not sure about that dress?" Gabi asked, coming up to her. Ferrin had been staring at the designer cocktail dress for too long. It was pricey but not out of her budget. It probably wasn't something she'd normally wear. She'd simply stopped next to it because she'd needed a break. A moment to let herself feel normal again instead of in this jet-set lifestyle that was Hunter's.

"I'm not. What do you think?" she asked, taking the dress from the rack and holding it up to herself. She shook off her thoughts. There was nothing she could do about the files while she was in San Francisco.

The dress was short, ending at midthigh, and had a halter neckline, which would leave her back bare. It was in her favorite color—turquoise—and made of a soft flowing synthetic fabric.

"Gorgeous! Kara, what do you think?" Gabi called to the other woman who had been discussing potty training with Ava, Christos's wife. Sheri, Tristan's wife, was in the dressing room trying on something that would in her words "make him forget I'm a mom and remember I'm a woman."

That had made them all laugh.

"Love it. You have to get it. Hunter is always so cool," Kara said. "You'll melt him in that gown."

"Try it on," Ava urged her. The four of them made their way to the dressing room just as Sheri came out in a strapless dress that looked as if it had been handmade for her.

"You have to get that," Kara said. "Tristan will definitely remember you from when you met and not as the mom of two boys."

"I agree," Gabi said. "One down, one to go."

"One to go? Do you mean me?" Ferrin asked.

"Yes. We all want to help you knock Hunter's socks off tonight," Gabi said, pushing her toward the dressing room.

She got in there and sat down on the bench, holding the dress in her lap. She knew that she had issues with men. There was a reason why her dream date involved sitting at home with *Pride and Prejudice* on the DVR and a pint of Ben and Jerry's Cherry Garcia in her hands. She didn't like to take risks.

Maybe it was because she didn't like to fail.

She glanced at her face in the mirror, trying to see the courage she always wanted to be there. But only her reflection was there. No secret courage came out of her eyes. If she wanted Hunter—and she admitted she did—she was going to have to show him and stop pushing him away.

Granted he had secrets—hell, everyone did. But the man she was coming to know she liked. She didn't want to have to keep a distance between them anymore. And honestly, when was she ever going to have the chance to go out with a man like him again?

She shucked off her clothes and turned away from the mirror so she wouldn't see herself in her underwear and pulled the dress on. It fit like a second skin as she got it into place and fastened the two tiny buttons at the back of her neck. She glanced over her shoulder in the mirror, checking her butt first. The skirt wasn't too tight, but her bra strap looked odd. She undid it and pulled it off, then turned to look at herself.

The dress was perfect. She liked the way it fit and the way she felt wearing it. She felt as if she could do anything. She stood on her toes to see if it would look better with heels, and it did fall a little differently on her body.

Tonight she decided she would stop pushing Hunter away. She'd take what she wanted and then tomorrow she'd offer him access to the files and see what happened. No more hiding and waiting.

"You coming out?"

"Just a second," Ferrin called.

She opened the dressing room door and poked her head out to find Gabi standing next to Kara. The two women were conversing in Spanish and stopped when they saw her. Ava and Sheri had walked back in and froze in their tracks.

"You have to get that dress," Ava said. "You look like an heiress."

"She does. I think if Tristan sees you, he might think you could be on the cover of our magazine," Sheri said.

"Okay, that's enough, ladies. I know what I look like. I admit the dress is nice, but I'm still me."

"Me is enough," Gabi said. "You are gorgeous, Ferrin."

Kara nodded. "My girls will think you're a secret princess going to a ball."

"It's not a long gown."

"It doesn't have to be," Kara said.

"True," Sheri agreed. "Hunter will never know what hit him."

"This is going to be the best night," Gabi added.

"Agreed. Now get changed back into your normal clothes and I'll take you all to my favorite lingerie shop so we can drive the men mad all night."

Ferrin purchased the dress and then spent more than she wanted for a pair of sexy heels and lingerie. It was probably the best shopping adventure she'd ever had in her life.

When she got back to Kara's house she looked around for Hunter but couldn't find him. She was distracted by the girls, who wanted to see her dress and came into the guest bedroom with her to touch it and ooh and aah over it. But she was worried about Hunter.

This seemed fun but only if she were with him. And she didn't want to face his friends if he wasn't here.

But she got dressed and came downstairs at six when they were supposed to leave for dinner. When she spotted Hunter standing there in a dinner jacket, she stopped at the top of the stairs.

Seeing him with his neatly trimmed beard and trousers that were cut to fit him took her breath away. He smiled up at her.

"You look beautiful."

"Thanks, handsome, you're not bad yourself," she said, coming down the stairs, determined to enjoy this night and this man and figure out what to do next.

Eight

Seconds nightclub was glamorous and Ferrin really didn't feel as though she belonged there. But all of Hunter's friends were busy trying to make her feel that she did. Gabi and Kingsley took turns telling her amusing tales about Hunter from back in his college days. And as the evening wore on they headed home early to check on Conner.

Sheri's dress had done the trick and Tristan had taken her into his arms as soon as they arrived. They'd been pressed together on the dance floor ever since.

Hunter had been talking with Gui and Christos about bringing his charity to Europe and maybe sponsoring some rugby leagues over there, and Ferrin had found herself chatting with Ava and Kara.

Hunter walked toward her as if drawn by something

other than his own will. As if instinct propelled him to her. She'd been talking to Ava in the corner, and was throwing her head back to laugh at something the other woman said when she noticed him.

He held his hand out to her and she took it. He pulled her to her feet and into his arms as the music swirled around them. The song was "Earned It (Fifty Shades of Grey)" by The Weeknd. The song's lyrics were raw and earthy and made her think of sex every time she heard them.

The music had the kind of sensual beat that started a fire deep inside her. One it seemed that Hunter shared, as well.

"Are you having fun tonight?" he asked, smoothing his hands and pulling her into the curve of his body as they swayed to the music.

"I am. I really like your friends," she said.

"They like you, too," he said. "But not as much as I do."

He tangled his hands in the back of her hair, pulling her head back and kissing her. She felt the touch of his mouth as he trailed his kisses down her neck. Shivers of desire coursed through her body. Her breasts felt fuller and an ache pulsed between her legs.

She wrapped her hand around the back of his neck and went up on tiptoe, biting the bottom of his earlobe and whispering what she wanted to do to him when they were alone.

He shuddered in her arms and danced them back into a secluded corner where no one could see them.

"Now, about ripping my clothes off," he said in a teasing voice.

She ran her hands down the front of his chest and undid the buttons over his flat stomach so she could reach her hand inside and caress him. His muscles fluttered under her touch and she pushed her finger lower, under the waistband of his pants.

Her finger rubbed over the tip of his erection and she leaned up again and bit his neck lightly.

He groaned her name and pulled her hand from his shirt. "I should have known better than to start something with you here. If you don't stop I'm going to come in my pants."

"You should have," she said with a grin. She stroked his length through the fabric of his dress pants. Cupping the back of his head, she drew his mouth to hers and kissed him long and hard and deep. It was the kind of kiss they'd been dancing around for days.

She'd been afraid before now to give in to her desires, but tonight seemed the perfect time for it. Most of her doubts about Hunter had faded and she was starting to fall for him.

He wrapped his arm around her, pulled her close, one hand on the side of her breast and the other one on her face. He tipped her head to the side as he brought his mouth down on hers.

His tongue slowly thrust deep into her mouth. He tasted so good. She sucked on his tongue and realized she wanted more. She shouldn't have started this in such a public place because she was pretty close to saying the hell with it and taking him here.

She grabbed his buttocks and pulled him more fully into her body, arching herself against him.

His breath was hot and sent another shaft of desire straight through her. She felt a drop of moisture between her legs and throbbed with longing.

He backed her up against the wall and she felt his thigh between her legs. He put one hand on her butt and urged her forward. He rocked his leg against her and she felt those tiny pulses spread up from her center through her body. She opened her eyes and all she saw was Hunter, watching her with a heated look that made everything else disappear.

She thrust her hips forward and felt another one of those tiny sensations and then he put his mouth on hers and with his hand on her butt urged her to move back and forth on his leg. She rocked against him until she felt the beginnings of her orgasm wash over her. Hunter swallowed her cries in his mouth and lifted his head only after she'd stopped rocking against him.

He lowered his leg to the floor and rubbed his hand down her back. She opened her eyes and looked at him. Felt his erection still hard between them. She reached for it but he drew her hand back.

"No. Not here. I want to wait until we are alone," he said.

She nodded, putting her head back against the wall and looking at Hunter. He made her feel alive in a way she never had before. Until this moment she wouldn't have said she was just skating through life but now she knew she had been. He squeezed her hand and rubbed his thumb over her lower lip.

"You are incredible," he said.

For the first time in her life she felt as if she was enough for a man.

The night had been so full of faces, music and wine. Her head was full of so many thoughts and her heart too much emotion.

She sat close to Hunter in the back of the limo he'd hired. There had been a crazy crush of photographers when they'd left the club and she knew they'd called to Hunter and to her and she'd waved at them as they'd gone past.

Now they were alone in the car and Hunter…he seemed distracted.

"I had a lovely time. Thank you for inviting me," she said. "Your friends are so charming. But I confess I had a very difficult time understanding Gui's accent."

"They adored you, too," Hunter said, putting his finger under her chin and tipping her head back. "But I can't blame them. It's easy to fall under your spell."

"Said the pot to the kettle."

He gave her a half smile, but it didn't look genuine. Something was nagging at him.

"Was it the photographers?"

"Was what?"

"Whatever is bothering you," she said. "I know you like your privacy." She put her head back against the plush leather seat and stared at the lights in the ceiling of the car. "I felt very glamorous when we walked out and there were all those flashbulbs going off."

"Did you?" he asked.

She turned her head without lifting it. "Yes, I did. I'm sorry they were there."

"Me, too," he said. "I wanted you all to myself. I should have listened to my instincts and taken you to my family's ranch in Texas instead of a nightclub."

"You were contemplating taking me to Texas?"

"Yeah," he said, taking her hand in his. "I like you, Ferrin."

She turned to face him, taking both of his hands in hers. "I like you, too, Hunter."

He smiled. A real smile this time, and she couldn't help but smile back. Tonight she felt she had gotten a glimpse of Hunter in his environment. Not the nightclub so much as with his friends. He'd relaxed. They'd spent the entire night behind the velvet rope in the VIP section and it had been eye-opening.

She thought she might write an article about it for *Psychology* magazine. She had a new insight. Of course, the insight could be due to all the wine she'd drunk.

"You know, I could limit myself to one glass of wine if I didn't like the taste of it so much."

He chuckled.

"Feeling the effects?" he asked. "Maybe that's why you thought the paparazzi were so exciting."

"Maybe. I just feel alive," she said. "I don't know if it's being back at Coach's house or him almost dying, but I've felt trapped in gloom for a while now." She glanced over at him. "I'm like a butterfly coming out of my cocoon."

"Okay, you definitely had too much vino, butterfly."

"Ha!" she said.

He hit a button and the sunroof opened. The crisp evening air flooded the car. She turned her face toward it and sighed. There were times when the wind felt so good on her face.

She shifted again and then remembered something she'd always wanted to do. "Is it illegal to stick your head out the sunroof?"

"Yes. Are you feeling wild tonight?" he asked.

She nodded.

He sighed and then shrugged out of his suit jacket. The action pulled his dress shirt tight across his muscled chest and she just stared at him. Now lust was taking over. Rather than sticking her head out the roof of a car, she'd like to have sex with Hunter.

She knew her time in California was drawing to a close. Her father had made as much of a recovery as he could with her help. And she needed to get back to her real life. She wanted to believe that the nightclub and the famous people who were there were her fairy tale but Hunter wasn't a prince. Or more precisely he wasn't *her* prince, and she needed to go back to her real life and remember that.

But for tonight...

Tonight she was going to take everything she could. There was no reason not to. She'd lived long enough to know that a moment like this wasn't going to come along again.

"Why are you watching me?"

"You're gorgeous," she said. "Surely you know that. When you get dressed in the morning you have to see all those perfectly sculpted muscles."

He blushed.

Oh, my God. He was embarrassed that she'd called him out on his body. He was too cute.

She knew that it wasn't just alcohol giving this night the magical feel. It was real.

"I don't."

"Yeah, the blush gave it away. You have to know you're hot," she said.

"Do you?" he asked.

"What? No. But I'm totally not. I'm just a psych professor, not a modern-day prince—I meant gladiator."

"I'm not a prince," he said.

"Tonight you are," she replied.

He held his hand out to her as he got to his feet and drew her up next to him. He wrapped his arm firmly around her waist as they poked their heads through the sunroof. They were on a side road, winding their way slowly back to Carmel-by-the-Sea, and the moon was a crescent over them. They were the only car on the road.

Hunter shifted so he was behind her. He braced his arms on each side of her as they moved slowly up the road. She felt safer than she ever had before. She tipped her head back and closed her eyes. She didn't know if this was love. But it was the closest she'd ever felt to something like this and she wanted it to last forever.

"Hey, you two," the driver yelled. "Back in the car."

Ferrin started laughing and Hunter pulled her back down on the seat next to him.

"Sorry. Bucket list," Hunter said.

"It's usually teenagers that do dumb stuff like that,"

the driver said, putting the window up between them again.

"Bucket list?"

"Yeah, I figured it was the only thing that made sense."

"Nothing makes sense," she replied. "I'm going on what feels right."

"And what is it that feels right to you?"

"This." She straddled his lap and put her hands on the seat behind him as she lowered her head and kissed him.

Nine

Hunter had a lap full of willing woman and a conscience full of guilt. But she had enchanted him tonight. Everyone had said she was too good for him in the club but in that way that friends and family do that means don't let this one go. But he couldn't keep her.

He knew that.

God, she tasted good. He should do the right thing and end this but he was tired of walking away from Ferrin.

He wanted her.

It had nothing to do with the past or Coach or anything other than that he liked being with her and she made him wish he were the man she thought he was. That would be nice.

Her tongue pushed deep into his mouth as she angled her head for deeper penetration. Her unique taste mingled with the flavor of the wine she'd had earlier.

She shifted her hips, rocking over his crotch, and his erection hardened. He widened his legs to make room for it and she sank lower against him.

He put his hand on her back, drawing her closer to him as he deepened the kiss. Her skin was soft and smooth under his hand. All night long he'd been tempted by that low-cut back on her dress. He traced the smooth expanse and skimmed his finger along the edge where fabric met flesh. She moaned a little, deep in her throat, and shifted back on her heels.

Her lips were swollen and wet from their kiss as she reached between them and pulled off his tie. She tossed it on the seat next to them.

"Do you mind?"

"Go ahead," he said, stretching his arms out on the back of the seat.

She slowly undid the buttons of his shirt, taking her time to make sure she was careful about getting them all. Just a thin line of his chest was visible now.

She took the sides of the shirt in her hand and then shifted forward again, rubbing her breasts against his chest as she kissed the side of his neck and slowly nibbled her way up to his ear.

He felt her hot breath against his skin and he was on fire. His erection was rock hard and his skin felt as if it was going to explode if he didn't feel her soft and naked pressed against him.

"What are you waiting for?" he asked.

"You to get over your shyness," she said, nipping at his earlobe. "I saw that blush earlier."

He laughed.

During sex.

He'd never had this kind of lightness in life. Ever. It just wasn't him, but Ferrin was once again showing him things about himself he didn't know.

"I'm okay," he said.

"I'll decide that."

She bit his neck and shifted to his other side. Sensation spread down his body. The fabric of his trousers drew tight against his erection and he reached between their bodies to undo his pants, lowering the zipper so he had room.

He pushed the skirt of her dress up and slipped his hands underneath, groaning when he cupped her naked buttocks.

"You're not wearing underwear?" he asked. His voiced sounded guttural even to his own ears.

"A thong," she said. "I'm a lady."

He groaned again as she bit his other ear and then pushed her hands under his open shirt. She spread her fingers and rubbed them over his pecs and then up to his shoulders, pushing the fabric off as her nails dug lightly into his flesh.

He arched his hips and groaned with a little bit of frustration. He reached lower to free himself and then, using his grip on her buttocks, pulled her down into full contact with him.

Yeah, that felt good.

He couldn't stop rubbing himself against her center,

and she shifted back on her heels, moaning as she gyrated against him. He ran his finger down the line of the fabric of her thong and felt her shudder in his arms.

She steadied herself against his shoulders as she rocked back and forth against him. She reached back, tried to brace herself on his knees but couldn't. She lost her balance and fell against him.

He wrapped his arms around her, holding her to him for a moment to catch his breath. He'd never felt this alive…this out of control. Well, not for a long time.

He moved his hands from under her dress to her back. With a quick twist of his fingers, the fabric fell away, revealing her naked breasts. Her nipples were pointed and hard, begging for his touch. He leaned forward, licking one before she scooted off his lap. She reached under her dress and pushed her thong down her legs and onto the floor and then shimmied out of the dress. She reached for the thigh-high hose but he stopped her.

"Leave them."

She nodded and then climbed back onto his lap. He felt her naked and ready against his erection and groaned.

"Are you on the pill?" he asked.

"Yes," she said. "Do you have a condom?"

"No, is that a problem?" he asked.

She hesitated, and then shook her head.

"Good," he said, pulling her closer to him. She settled over him again. He caressed both of her arms, slowly moving from her shoulders down to her wrists.

She had such long, lovely limbs. He took her hands and placed them on the heels of her shoes.

"Hold on to your ankles for balance," he said.

She tried it and grinned down at him. "That works."

It also kept her hands off him so he might have a few moments to regain his control. Because he was about to lose it like a teenager alone with a girl for his first time.

Overcome, he wrapped his arms around her and drew her close to him. He lowered his head between her breasts and it was only the feel of her fingers in his hair that pulled him out of the emotional trap that he'd been sliding toward. Later, he'd figure that out, but right now there were more pressing matters that demanded his full attention.

He turned his head to the right and found her nipple, sucking it deep into his mouth. She arched her back, rubbing her core against his erection, and he groaned as he felt her heat on his naked flesh.

He shifted his hips and felt the tip of him at the opening of her body. She braced her hands on his shoulders and slowly slid down him. He tore his mouth from her breast and looked up at her. Her breasts were thrust forward and her eyes half-closed as she took him as deeply as she could, sinking all the way down on him. She leaned forward and thrust her fingers into his hair as her mouth found his. She sucked his tongue deep into her mouth as she started to move on him.

So slowly. She rocked back and forth. Her nipples rubbed against his chest and he cupped her butt, hoping to speed her up. But then he realized that he wanted this moment, this night to last forever.

He dug his fingers into her butt cheeks and held her fiercely to him as she arched her back and rocked on him.

He leaned forward to capture one nipple in his mouth as he ran his finger along the furrow between her cheeks, and she shivered in his arms and her hips started to move more quickly. She shifted her thighs farther apart and took him deeper into her body. He felt himself growing bigger inside her. He was so tight that he knew he was seconds from his orgasm. He rocked her harder against him, took her deeper and deeper, until she shook and shuddered in his arms. He felt her pulsing around him and then he held her closely to him and thrust up into her hard and fast until he reached his own climax.

He kept thrusting until he was empty and then Ferrin fell forward in his embrace, her head on his shoulder and her arms limply by her sides. He hugged her to him, holding her and stroking her back with one hand. The sunroof was still open and the cool night breeze helped to dry the sweat on his body.

Ferrin kissed his shoulder and then turned her head until their eyes met. She glanced up at him with a dreamy look in her eyes and he felt a punch in the gut. He wished like hell that this was real. That he could keep her. Because for the first time since he'd lost everything he had something he wanted.

Someone he needed.

He wanted to be the man she thought he was so that she'd always look up at him this way.

He tangled his hand in her hair and kissed her hard

and deep. She moaned a little and then bit his lower lip. "That was incredible. Thank you. I guess that's two I can check off tonight."

She shifted off his lap and next to him on the seat. He reached into his pocket and took out the handkerchief that his father always insisted men carry and handed it to her to clean up.

"What do you mean, two?"

"Off my bucket list," she said, delicately wiping between her legs before drawing her dress to her and putting it back on. He tucked himself back in his pants but left his shirt off and his pants undone. He just didn't want to do anything that would take away from this moment. He tugged Ferrin off balance and drew her back into the curve of his body.

He knew that he should just let her sit over there and put her barriers back up, and hell, he should definitely be putting his guard back in place.

He kissed the top of her head.

"What else is on your bucket list?" he asked.

She shifted around until her legs were stretched out on the rest of the seat and put her hands over his arm where he held her. She stroked his fingers over his forearm and made a soft sighing sound as she did so.

"I don't know. I mean, travel, right? Everyone wants to travel."

"I don't."

"You don't?" she asked, tipping her head back to see his face.

"Nope. I traveled a lot in my playing days. And there isn't any place I can't afford to go."

"Fair enough. But I am saving for Fiji. I want to take my mom and stepdad there. They wanted to go on their honeymoon but they are teachers so that wasn't happening," she said. "That is definitely on my bucket list."

"That sounds like your mom's bucket list, not yours," Hunter said.

"It is. But I love her so it's on mine, too."

He hugged her close. He'd checked something off his bucket list tonight, too. But would he be able to hold on to Ferrin much longer?

Ten

"Hey, we're here," Hunter said, gently shaking Ferrin's shoulder. She'd fallen asleep in his arms and for a moment he'd felt some kind of peace, a contentment that he'd never experienced before. It weirded him out.

He didn't want Ferrin to have this power over him, but he knew it was too late and she did.

The driver opened the door and Ferrin sleepily got out of the car. Hunter climbed out next to her and draped his jacket over her shoulders. He tipped the driver and joined her as he drove away.

"This isn't Coach's house," she said.

"I know. Joy's not expecting you until morning and I really don't want the night to end yet," Hunter said. "If you want to go home, I'll take you."

She wrapped her arms around his waist and rested

her head in the center of his chest. "I don't want this night to end either."

"Good," he said. He rubbed his hands up and down her back, and she was holding him as though she never wanted to let him go.

He hadn't realized how much he'd needed that until this moment.

He glanced up at the sky. It would be sunrise soon. He tugged on her hand and drew her up the walkway to his front door. He entered the code to unlock it. Once inside in his foyer, he scooped her up and carried her up the stairs to his bedroom. The lights were on a motion sensor and came on as he passed them.

"That's cool with your lights," she said.

He smiled at that. "I'm afraid of the dark."

"You aren't, are you?"

"Not really afraid. I just don't like being alone in a dark house. So my mom sent me these lights when I moved in."

"She knows?" Ferrin asked.

"Yeah, you know how moms are. They are the keeper of all secrets," he said. "Like my older brother is afraid of butterflies. He thinks they're creepy and won't go into a garden that features them."

Ferrin started laughing. "How do you know that?"

"Mom. She was trying to cheer me up," Hunter admitted. "She shared Nate's fear when I was just released from jail and had been struggling to deal with Stacia's death." There had been no time to grieve for her in the immediate aftermath of learning about her death because he'd been carted off to jail. It was only after he'd been released that her death had started to sink in. He'd been in so much pain, his guilt so heavy.

"Your mother sounds wonderful."

"She is," Hunter said. He couldn't believe he'd just said something to Ferrin about Stacia's death. Ever since their first date when he'd explained the past, he'd remained tightlipped about it, and Ferrin had respected his silence.

He put Ferrin on her feet next to his bed. "I… It was a really dark time in my life."

"I'm sorry you had such a dark patch," Ferrin said. She shrugged out of his suit jacket and handed it to him. Then she lay down on his bed.

He sighed. Her hair fanned out around her head like some sort of ethereal angel's and she ran her arms back and forth over the thick quilt that covered his bed.

"Ferrin—"

"Don't."

"Don't what?"

"Talk about the real world. I know this night is just, well, tonight. It's magical and special and I don't want anything to spoil it."

Hunter wanted that, too. He tossed his jacket over the back of the armchair he kept in his room for reading and then fell back on the bed next to her. She held his hand and squeezed it.

"Thank you," she said, quietly.

"You're welcome," he said. He rolled onto his side and stared down at her.

"Want to have a bath?" he asked. "After the night out and a long car ride it might be nice."

"It would be," she said.

"Stay here," he said, dropping a quick kiss on her lips as he pushed himself off the bed. He entered his bathroom and turned on the lights over the large hot tub. It took him a few minutes to get everything set up. He made sure he had a robe for Ferrin to wear when they got out and thick towels for both of them. Then he went back into the bedroom and found her sleeping in the middle of his bed.

He watched her for a long moment. Stared down at her sleeping face and felt that punch to the heart that he had been trying to ignore for too long.

It was hard to keep his guard up, to keep Ferrin from mattering as much as she did to him. But until he knew the truth about Stacia's murder, falling for Ferrin was a mistake. He still needed access to whatever her father had in his office. But as Hunter looked down at her... his heartbeat sped up and he admitted he needed Ferrin more.

He carefully reached underneath her and unfastened her dress. He drew it down her body and then carried it to his closet, putting it on a hanger and getting one of his white T-shirts for her to wear. He put it on her and shifted her up to one of the pillows and tucked her into his bed.

Ferrin woke with a start. There was a heavy arm around her stomach and a man curled up against her back.

Hunter.

She'd fallen asleep while he'd been drawing a bath

for them. He was warm and he held her in a way she'd always wanted to be held. She felt safe and protected. But something had woken her.

What?

She glanced at the clock on the nightstand and saw it was almost seven in the morning. Last night had been one of the most fun she'd had as an adult. She'd never thought she'd be partying with football players and jet-setters but she had.

And she'd found that behind the glitz, glamour and paparazzi they were nice people. She'd enjoyed it a lot.

She carefully lifted Hunter's arm and climbed out of his bed. She used the bathroom and got a drink of water from the bottle next to the sink and then put the lid down on the toilet and sat on it.

She was punching above her weight with Hunter. They were very different people with very different lives.

But she'd come to a decision.

She put her elbows on her knees and rested her head in her hand. The music from the nightclub was still beating in her mind and she knew that she'd never forget it. Not a single moment of it.

She wasn't getting closer to her dad and honestly, after last night, seeing the pain that Hunter was still in over Stacia's unsolved murder, Ferrin couldn't hold out any longer. From everything Hunter had ever told her, he was innocent. If he could prove it by going through a bunch of old tapes and papers in her dad's office, she was going to let him.

And then she'd say goodbye to her dad, Hunter and the West Coast and go back to her normal life.

One night in the castle was all this fairy-tale princess was allowed. Just one night. She knew that once Hunter got what he wanted from her, he'd lose interest. But she was fine with that.

Wasn't she?

"Ferrin? You okay?"

She glanced up to see Hunter standing in the doorway. He wore only a pair of boxer briefs and had one arm braced against the doorjamb. His hair was tousled and his eyes were sleepy.

"Yes, I was just thirsty. Sorry I conked out on you," she said.

"I'm surprised you made it as long as you did. Want to come back to bed?" he asked.

She stood up. "I do, but first, you wanted to talk earlier and I shut you down. I'm sorry about that."

"It's okay," he said.

He held his hand out to her and she hesitated. Maybe it was the hour or maybe it was reality starting to creep back into the magic of the night, but she didn't just go to him the way she would have a few hours ago.

He let his hand drop to his side and stood there looking so alone. Almost afraid. She wished she'd just gone to him. But the fairy-tale magic of the night was waning and she was starting to feel like her old self again.

"What is it?" he asked.

"Tonight just brought home how different our lives are and I thought...well, I thought if you told me something else I was going to have to admit I don't belong here with you."

He walked into the bathroom, padding carefully over to her. "I think we do belong together, Ferrin. I think that's the reason why both of us are so afraid to let reality intrude. But maybe all of that isn't important. I know that we've only known each other a short while, but I care for you."

Her heartbeat sped up. She cared for him, too. "It feels too fast, doesn't it?"

"Not to me. But then I'm used to making decisions at lightning speed and rolling with the tackles. You were unexpected," he said.

"I was?" she asked. It sounded sweet to her. She knew he'd started out trying to seduce something out of her. And she'd let him. Because it was a hell of a lot more fun to enjoy flirting with Hunter than fighting with him over access to her father's stuff. And pretty early on, Hunter had even stopped pushing her on that issue, giving her time and space to make up her own mind.

"You were and still are. I thought I had a solid game plan. I thought I knew exactly what I was going to do, but you've managed to make me rethink it," he said.

"How?" she asked.

Instead of answering, he wrapped one arm around her hips and picked her up. He carried her back into the bedroom and tossed her on the bed, following her down onto it. He lay on top of her, his body braced on his elbows, his hands framing her face.

He rested his forehead against hers and the expression in his eyes scared her with its intensity.

But he blinked before she could analyze it. He rubbed his lips over hers and gave her a soft, sleepy kiss that banished all her questions and worries.

He held himself over her on the bed, just the heat of his body and his lips touching her. He thrust his tongue deep into her mouth and she moaned as she arched underneath him. She wrapped her arms around him and traced the muscles of his back as he lifted his head.

He tangled his hands in her hair, tugging softly until she arched her neck so that he could kiss the length of it. His soft beard tickled her neck and sent chills through her body. Her nipples tightened and she felt an aching emptiness between her legs. She spread them and his hips settled in between.

She felt the ridge of his hard-on press against her. She undulated under him, rubbing her center against his hardness. Her head twisted on the pillow as he sucked on the pulse that beat frantically at the spot where her neck and collarbone met.

More shivers coursed through her and she felt a drop of moisture between her legs as the heat he was generating in her spread all over. She skimmed her fingers down his sides, stretching to reach his buttocks and pull him closer to her. He rotated his hips so that the tip of his erection rubbed over her and she moaned.

She felt his breath hot against her neck. His chest slid over her breasts as he moved against her. The soft cotton T-shirt was a nuisance, a barrier between them that she wanted out of the way, but she'd have to let go of him to move it and he felt so good everywhere.

She didn't want to stop touching him. To stop caressing his firm buttocks or his back. She drew her fingernail up the length of it, tracing the line of his spine, and his hips jerked forward as he bit her neck.

He shifted a little on her, pushing the T-shirt she wore up until her breasts were bare. He leaned on one elbow, keeping his erection pressed against her center, and caressed her breast with his hand. Her nipple pebbled as he drew his finger around it. Just circling her areola; not touching it really, simply teasing her.

She arched her back, trying to nudge his hand where she wanted it, but he wouldn't be hurried. He leaned over her and she felt the heat of his breath on her nipple. It grew firmer before his lips closed over it. He flicked at her with his tongue and she shivered and shuddered in his arms.

He lifted his head and rubbed his cheek against her breast. The softness of his beard abraded her, sending tingles down her body, and she felt everything feminine inside her go on red alert. She dug her heels into the bed and arched against him, rubbing herself against the ridge of him, and he rotated his hips in response.

He held her with one hand on her shoulder as he shifted to his knees between her legs and slowly kissed his way down the center of her body to her belly button. He flicked his tongue into it and she tightened. He nipped at her, rubbed his beard stubble against her and slowly worked his way from one side of her body to the other.

She put her hands on his head and tried to draw him up her body so that she could have him inside her again. But he wouldn't be budged. He draped her thighs over his shoulders and parted her intimate flesh with his fingers.

His breath was warm against her and then she felt the flick of his tongue on her. She shuddered and cried out, her thighs jerking together on each side of his head. He flicked his tongue over her again and she arched in his arms. She felt the touch of his finger as he traced the opening of her body and then slowly pushed his finger up inside her. She was shivering as the first waves of orgasm rocked through her but she knew she wanted more than he was giving her. She didn't want him to stop. Her head thrashed back and forth on the bed as he continued to eat at her most intimate flesh and she couldn't stop the climax that shook her.

She grabbed the back of his head, holding him to her as she arched up against his face. He licked her until she calmed down and then shifted back, letting her legs fall to the bed. He freed his erection and crawled up over her body, pushing her legs farther apart as he entered her. He drove himself deep inside and she tightened around him.

He drew his hips back and started driving into her, building her up once more. Even though she wasn't sure she'd come again, she did. She trembled underneath him, digging her nails into his back until she felt him thrusting faster and harder, and then she heard his groan as he found his own release.

She arched underneath him again, wrapping her

arms around him and holding him close until he collapsed on her. He rolled to his back, pulling her with him. He held her in his arms and she felt herself drifting off. She didn't want to sleep yet. She wanted to watch him sleep. But she couldn't stop herself. He held her close, covering them both with the quilt, and she felt safe in his arms.

She returned the embrace, feeling for the first time that she'd found something she hadn't known she'd been searching for. She'd found something in Hunter that made her feel no matter how different they were they could overcome all obstacles.

When they woke in the morning, she put last night's dress back on and Hunter drove her home. She stood in the doorway and watched until his car wasn't visible anymore before going into the house.

She hadn't had a chance to tell him about her decision to let him go through Coach's stuff. But once she showered she would. It was a late summer day with the sun shining down. This was the kind of day where anything was possible, she thought. Anything at all.

Eleven

As she walked through the house, Ferrin hummed the song that had been on in the car when Hunter dropped her off. She had her shower and then went into the kitchen where Joy had prepared his breakfast tray. Joy wasn't in the room, so Ferrin took it and went upstairs.

"Hello, sunshine." Her father's voice was a little stronger this morning. After their lunch downstairs before she'd gone to San Francisco, he'd relapsed. He wouldn't leave his room and he scarcely spoke to her.

Ferrin set the tray down on the side table and went to open the drapes.

"Good morning, Dad. How are you feeling?" she asked.

"Better. What did you do yesterday?" he asked.

She picked up his tray and brought it over to him. She plumped the pillows behind him.

"I spent the day in San Francisco with a friend," she said.

Why was she reluctant to mention Hunter's name? *Lying.* She really didn't have the stomach for it. Maybe she was imagining that her father would have a negative reaction. But she didn't want to talk about Hunter until she figured out if the feelings she had for him were real.

They felt real. To be honest she had a hard time not thinking about him as she'd had her shower and then gotten dressed to come and visit her dad.

It was a new day but the magic of the night before seemed to cling to her. For the first time she felt as if she'd found a man she could trust. And if she wasn't mistaken, Hunter felt the same about her. She thought back to the way he'd held her last night, keeping her close to him, as if he never wanted to let her go.

"That's nice. Did you have a good time?" Coach asked.

"I did," she said, perching on the edge of the guest chair and sipping her coffee.

"Dad?"

"Yes."

"Hunter Caruthers has asked to be able to go through boxes of stuff sent over from the college. He's looking for a videotape that was in one of the boxes. Would that be okay?"

"What boxes?" he asked. His eyes looked a little cloudy and it was easy to read the confusion on his face.

"Just some old files and videotapes from your coaching days. I'd like to pick some things to give back to the college for your tribute. Someone from the college was asking for that, too."

"I don't want the tribute," he said. "Who called from the college?

"Ferrin?"

"Sorry, Coach," she said. "It was the acting head of the football program, Graham Peters."

"Graham Peters. That boy doesn't know a pig from a pigskin. I can't believe they want him to organize a tribute to me."

"Well, we could have more input if you'd let me go through the boxes. Maybe I'll ask a few of your former players to come and help me. I feel like those men know you best."

Once Hunter had a look in the boxes she'd know if he was sticking around for her.

But a part of her felt as if last night had changed that. That he was no longer here because of practice tapes or old files. They'd had sex—soul sex, she thought. She hoped it was the same for him.

But she was afraid to trust her feelings. Afraid to believe she was enough for Hunter. And as she glanced at the big man in the bed, her father the coach, she knew that was the legacy of their broken relationship.

If she were alone she would have probably cursed. But she wasn't. She was waiting for her father's answer.

"Some of the players? Have they been by to see me?" he asked.

"Yes. But when you're not feeling well, we turn them away."

He was very lucid and there was an expression on

his face that she really couldn't identify. She wished now she'd never asked. If he said no what was she going to do?

"No."

"Dad—"

"I don't want to rehash the past. I already told the college and I'm telling you, I'm not going to do it."

She found it hard to reconcile the man who had a trophy room downstairs to this man who was pushing his fruit salad around on his plate and saying he didn't want to be honored for the sport he loved.

"You spent your life pursuing this," she said, quietly. "I wish I could understand this decision."

He put his fork down and turned his head away from her and for the first time she saw her father as a man. Not the demanding, larger-than-life coach he'd always been but someone fallible with feet of clay.

"I'm not that man anymore," he said. "Why is it so important to you? I know you don't care about football or another award for me."

"You're right, I don't. I just want to feel like all those years you chose football over me were worth it. I want to maybe see something in your coaching years and those teams that you gave all your time to that will make me understand why I wasn't good enough."

She got to her feet and strode to the door. She'd said too much. She knew Coach didn't like emotional outbursts.

"Ferrin."

"What?" she asked.

"I was the one who couldn't measure up, not you," he said.

She wanted to believe him but a lifetime of being second best made it really hard. "I wish that were true."

He cursed and she opened the door to step out into the hallway. She wasn't sure what she'd expected. A part of her, the lost little girl inside her, felt a little relief at what he'd said, but the adult—the woman—knew the words were too little, too late.

Joy waited at the bottom of the stairs. The housekeeper looked worried.

"Are you okay?" Ferrin asked, hurrying over to her.

"Yes, I was watching *E! News Daily* while I made your father's breakfast," she said.

"Did one of the celebrities you follow die?" Joy was seriously into the people she followed. She talked about them as though they were her friends and family. When Justin Bieber started having trouble with the law, she had been very upset. She'd thought he needed a hug and a good talking-to.

"No. That's not it," Joy said. "Ferrin, you know that player who stopped by to see your father… Hunter Caruthers?"

"Yes. He's the friend I went to San Francisco with. We had a really nice time," Ferrin said, not sure where Joy was going with this.

"Come into the kitchen," Joy said.

"You're freaking me out a little," Ferrin admitted. "What's up?"

"I was hoping that he would have just left us all alone or maybe told you himself," Joy said.

"What do you mean?"

"Do you remember ten years ago there was a coed murdered at the college? Two of your dad's players were arrested for the murder," Joy said. "Hunter was one of those men. His girlfriend was the woman they found dead."

"But the charges were dropped and he was released. Hunter told me all about this. He's innocent."

Joy looked confused. "I'm sorry. I just… I saw you both leaving Seconds on *E! News Daily* and I realized… well, I was afraid you didn't know. And the reporter said the authorities were thinking of reopening the case against Hunter. There's new evidence that he broke up with the murdered girl right before she was found dead. He's always claimed he was too drunk to remember what happened that night but people are now saying that was a lie."

Ferrin froze. Hunter had never told her that he broke up with Stacia. Granted, he hadn't told her much beyond the basic facts. Could it be that he was trying to get at her father's stuff to destroy the evidence instead of prove his innocence? A chill ran through her body.

"Thank you, Joy."

"It's okay, honey," she said. "I don't know much more beyond that."

"Thank you. I'm going up to my room."

"Do you want me to bring you anything? Maybe a cup of tea?" Joy asked.

"No," she said. She wasn't in the mood for tea. She

needed to process what she'd just learned. What did it mean? Could she really trust Hunter? And, for that matter, could she stand the harsh attention of the media that Hunter attracted? It was a stark reminder of how different their two worlds were.

She entered her bedroom. It had no reminders of her childhood since she'd barely spent two weeks here every year when she was growing up. She went to the armchair near the window and sat down. All the happiness she'd felt earlier had dried up. Gone.

Her phone buzzed and she glanced down at it. A text from Hunter.

Dammit, she didn't know what to say.

She tossed the phone on the bed and stared out the window. The sky was bright and sunny and in the distance she saw the ocean and the ragged coastal cliffs. If she stood at the window she'd be able to see the cove where she and Hunter had paddleboarded to.

She wasn't a California girl. She wanted to be back in her landlocked home in Texas with the big sky easily visible to her after just a short drive. Texas…that was where she was safe. Not here. Where everything was too complicated.

She had come to take care of her father because her conscience wouldn't let her do otherwise. But now she realized she was chasing something that she'd never get. Something that had always been as elusive as her ability to catch a football. She'd stumbled, fallen and fumbled the ball. There was no way to win this game, and she was throwing in the towel before she collected any more injuries.

She got to her feet, went to her closet and grabbed out her battered suitcase and packed it. She didn't hesitate or try to convince herself otherwise. She had to leave.

Run away.

She was a coward, she thought.

But was it cowardly to just protect herself. She'd fallen for Hunter. Hook, line and sinker. But he wasn't telling her the whole truth. Had he been playing her? And was it a deadly game?

Why was it so hard to fall in love with a decent man?

Had her father damaged her so much that she didn't think she deserved one? Even when she'd thought she'd found a man who was different…she was still the loser.

She picked up her phone, entered the code to open it and hit the button to call Hunter's number. She wanted to hear his voice when she asked him why. She didn't want a text message full of excuses or lies. Pass fake— that's what he'd told her about in football. But her eyes were open now and she wasn't about to let herself be distracted again.

Hunter hadn't gone far after he'd dropped Ferrin off, just driven down to the beach where they'd gone paddle-boarding and parked his car in the nearly empty parking lot. He saw a few battered cars that he assumed belonged to the surfers who were out catching waves before they had to go to their day jobs.

He put the seat back and his sunglasses on. He was tired and he had a headache. He had texted Ferrin just to see if she had seen the breaking news that he'd gotten an alert about on his phone from the ESPN app. But she didn't answer. He also sent a text to Kingsley warning him that they might never have access to Coach's old files now. Kingsley texted back that they would find the information another way. And then asked if he wanted to talk.

Hell, he did want to talk. To Ferrin. But he had no idea if she was going to talk to him ever again.

The reporter had all but implied that he and Kingsley were about to be rearrested. And though Hunter knew it was an exaggeration, what would Ferrin think? He hadn't told her the whole truth about Stacia and the breakup. About the guilt that prevented him from getting too close to any woman.

Until now.

His phone rang a few minutes later and he glanced at the caller ID.

Ferrin.

She knew.

He answered the phone. "Hello."

"I guess you know what I'm calling about," she said. He heard her voice tremble and then she took a deep breath.

"Can I see you? I feel like we should have this conversation in person."

"I don't think that's such a good idea. Is the report on TV true? Why didn't you tell me that you broke up with Stacia the night of the murder?"

"I couldn't. The shame is still too much for me to deal with, let alone talk about. That's why I need to access Coach's stuff. "

"Or are you trying to get to it to hide something?"

"How could you say that? Do you really think I killed Stacia?"

"I don't know what to think anymore. I'm just in way over my head and need some time to sort it out."

She disconnected the call.

He rubbed his hand over his chest. His gritty eyes stung so he pushed his sunglasses up on his forehead and rubbed them. The sun was bright today, seeming to mock him. But then California had never been great for him. He had moments of great triumph followed by...well, depths he hadn't ever anticipated. Maybe that was his problem.

He'd been busy working his game plan, trying to convince Ferrin to do what he wanted, and he'd screwed up. He should have realized with a woman like her he couldn't play a game.

He put his seat back into position and drove out of the parking lot. The traffic was starting to get heavier and he had to pay attention as he drove through a school zone and then by the community center that Gabi and Kingsley were building. He saw the seeds of the future there and knew he couldn't just drive away from Ferrin.

That's how he ended up at Ferrin's house.

It was no longer Coach's house to him. It was Ferrin's.

Hunter sat there on the street instead of parking in the driveway. He was tired. He'd had no time to plan but he had to see her. He had to explain.

His iPhone had a video feature and he thought that maybe if she saw him instead of just hearing his voice, she'd understand.

He took the phone out and used the front-facing camera. He looked rough and tired. Broken. And he was. Stacia's death had brought him to his knees and he would have thought that nothing else could. But this... this thing with Ferrin was another blow.

He hit Record and then nodded at his reflection.

"Ferrin, please don't hit Delete. I'm sorry. You're right, I should have told you everything I knew about that night..."

When he was done recording, he messaged the video to Ferrin. He waited, staring at the iMessage screen on his phone until he saw that it had been delivered and then read.

She'd read it. She'd opened his video. Did that mean she'd watched the entire thing? He didn't know.

But he'd sit here until he had a reply and then...well, then he'd make another plan. Because as much as he needed answers and closure about the past he needed to make this right with the woman who could very well be his future.

He saw someone walking toward the car.

Ferrin.

Twelve

Ferrin had no idea what she was going to say to Hunter when she saw him. But that video…

It made her believe that he was struggling, too. That he wanted, well, forgiveness. She wasn't sure she was ready for that. But she wanted to at least hear from his lips what had happened.

He opened his car door and now that she was so close to him, a mix of anger and fear roared up inside her again. It surprised her.

He got out, closed the door and crossed his arms over his chest. "I guess you got my video."

"I probably shouldn't even be down here right now. It was just that I needed to see you."

He didn't say anything, just dropped his arms to his sides.

"Here I am. You know me now, Ferrin. All the scars and battle wounds that I was trying to hide. The ugliness that I can't get rid of."

He dropped his head toward his chest and then shook it and lifted it back up again. She couldn't read his expression through the dark sunglasses he wore.

"Could we go someplace and talk about this? I don't think we should do it out here on the street," he said. "I'll answer all of your questions."

"Okay. Meet me at Café Carmel in town in thirty minutes."

"I can't go into a coffeehouse in Carmel," he said. "I'll be recognized. People will really gawk now that it's out they might be reopening the case. You remember how it was that first night when we went to dinner."

"I do remember."

"How about the beach? It's public but we can have some privacy, too," Hunter said.

"Okay. I'll get my car and follow you." She just didn't think she could handle being alone with him in a car right now.

"Stop being ridiculous. I'll drive you."

"No. I need to be able to leave on my own. Until you tell me the whole truth, it's not a good idea for me to be dependent on you for anything."

"Screw that, Ferrin. I'm hurt, too. I know it's my fault that you're mad. But that doesn't lessen my anger."

He took his sunglasses off and the rawness in his eyes made her stomach hurt. But she couldn't just let this go.

"There's a park at the end of the street. Want to go talk on the bench there?" she suggested.

He put his sunglasses back on and hit the lock button for his car. "Which way is the park?"

"This way," she said. She began walking down the street. When she'd visited her dad after her parents had divorced she'd spent a lot of time in the park. Swinging and pretending that if she could get the swing high enough she'd be able to escape from the reality of her life.

She'd tried really hard when she'd first started coming to visit him to be the daughter he wanted. She'd failed miserably.

Maybe that was why she kept failing with men in relationships. She couldn't be what a man wanted. She had to be what she wanted and then the right man would come along.

Hunter followed slowly behind her and she felt a little bit of her anger and confusion wane. He sat down next to her, leaving more than a respectable distance between them. This was it. He'd tell her whatever he thought would make him feel better about why he lied. She'd have to be grown up about it and then she'd send him on his way.

The crash landing from her time in the glamorous world of Hunter Caruthers hadn't entirely been unexpected. From the beginning she'd known they came from two very different worlds. But she'd had no idea how different.

And the crash wasn't the one she'd expected.

She crossed her legs and tried to be objective, the

way she counseled her students who were studying psychology. She wanted to find a label for Hunter and pin it to him, but her mind wasn't dominating her right now. Her heart was and she wasn't finding objectivity at all.

"So talk. Start from the beginning."

"Stacia and I met the first day I was on campus. I had been a big fish in a little pond back in Texas. Everyone thought I was destined for great things but it was scary to be in California. Everyone seemed like they belonged. And Stacia came over to me and offered me something…a cookie. She'd baked a bunch at home before driving down from Oregon."

"That's sweet," she said. She heard in his voice the affection and the guilt he felt toward Stacia. What *had* happened the night she died?

"It was. She'd grown up on a farm and her parents were into organic food. She taught me about juicing and kept me healthy with the meals she'd cook for me."

"Did you live together?"

"Nah, I was in the frat house and she lived in an apartment off campus to save money."

Ferrin was sad for the girl who never had a chance to be a woman. She sounded like someone Ferrin would have liked to know. And Hunter felt guilty about her death. Why?

He stretched his legs out in front of himself and stared off in the distance.

"She was taking nursing classes. Her mom was a nurse and all Stacia wanted to be was like her mom—" He broke off and turned away. He stared at the horizon and didn't say anything else and for once she had no idea what to say.

"What happened the night she died?" Ferrin finally asked. She wasn't sure what she'd hoped to hear in his voice. But aside from the affection and the guilt, she heard pain and sadness. She wasn't a judge or a jury. She wanted to pretend the reason she needed to know about his past was solely because of the files in her father's den, but she knew as a woman who cared for Hunter, she wanted answers. He wanted her to go against her father's wishes and give him access to papers and videos that for some reason her father wanted to hide.

Pushing his sunglasses up on his head, Hunter turned back to her, and the weighted expression in his eyes made the ache inside her deepen.

"I…it was the end of the season and rumor had it Kingsley was going to get the Heisman Trophy again. I was projected to be drafted by the NFL and I started to think of the future. Coach had talked to me and said I was too young to be tied down with a girlfriend. That being in the NFL was my chance to focus on playing."

"I can hear Coach saying that. Nothing's more important than the game. So you and Stacia had dated all through college?"

"Yeah, all four years. Senior year we weren't as close as we'd once been—I was busy with meetings and playing so we'd only been on a few dates and we were both feeling pulled away from each other," Hunter said.

But she wasn't too sure she wanted to hear more about this woman whom Hunter once loved. It would be foolish to be jealous of a dead woman but Ferrin wondered if Hunter was still in love with Stacia.

"I can see that. It's sad, Hunter. But what I need to know is if you took a drastic measure to get free."

"Well, I didn't kill her," Hunter said. "I thought you'd know that."

"I thought I did, too, but you sound guilty when you talk about her."

"Yeah, I broke up with her that night. Told her we needed time apart and things weren't working out. She got upset and we had a fight and she left the frat house. A bunch of people heard us fighting, which is why the cops originally suspected me."

"How does Kingsley play into that?" she asked. "I don't imagine he was fighting with her, as well."

"No, he wasn't. After Stacia left, Kingsley and I went to the living room and got drunk. I passed out and when I woke up the cops were at the door and we were both arrested."

"They arrested you?"

"Yes. Kingsley's brother is a big-time lawyer so he flew out to be with us when we were questioned. At first we didn't even know why we'd been arrested. When I heard that it was…that Stacia was dead… I couldn't—"

He turned away and put his head in his hands. Suddenly all the anger, fear and heartbreak drained away from her. She wasn't sure she could care about him the way she had last night but this man was broken. He couldn't have possibly killed Stacia.

Ferrin touched him. Just a brief light tap of his shoulder because her arms ached to hug him. The same way she'd have comforted a stranger in the street if she'd seen someone break down. Or at least that was what she really wanted to believe.

"Okay. So how is this related to Dad's stuff? What do you think you're going to find there?" she asked.

Hunter turned to face her. "I'm sorry about that. I haven't spoken out loud about Stacia in a long time. I wanted some closure for myself of course, but also for her. I want to know what happened that night and let her parents know. They deserve that. Your father's files and tapes might be another false lead, but I'm hoping that maybe there is something on the tapes that might explain what happened. Gabi was also a student at the time and she heard—hell, it sounds like gossip—but there's a chance someone on the team was drugging girls and then raping them. I'm not saying Coach knew anything about that but there might be something in his notes to help me find out."

She wrapped her arms around her waist. She hadn't known what to expect but she hadn't expected to feel this kind of empathy.

"Fair enough. I… I need to think about this," she said. "I'll go home and give you my answer in a few days."

She needed to know why her father was so adamantly opposed to letting Hunter see the boxes of stuff from his office. Did he know something? Was he protecting someone?

"I'm haunted, Ferrin. I have to exhaust every line of inquiry. I have to figure out what happened so that we can both have some peace. I hate that whatever happened back then has cost me twice."

A small group of moms and toddlers were walking toward the park and Hunter put his sunglasses back on. In Texas most people got behind him. After all he was a son of the Lone Star State and they had always believed in his innocence. But in California where the story had been played in the media nonstop until he and Kingsley had been released from jail, people thought that they'd bought their freedom.

Kingsley was the son of a wealthy family, as was Hunter. People called them the privileged elite and said that they thought they were better than the law. But they hadn't been. It was easy for people to assume that money fixed everything but it hadn't. It had simply given them the means to leave California. Hunter wouldn't have come back here if not for Kingsley.

But Kingsley had been tired of running. He wanted his son to grow up here and now that he and Gabi were engaged they wanted to make their life here. They deserved to do it free of suspicion and vicious tongues.

As much as Hunter needed to put the past to rest for himself.

"If I let you go through his stuff, that's it. I need to take a step back," she said. "When I heard that there was a story about us on E!, I realized everything is going way too fast." Her voice was level and calm but there was still a flush on her cheeks.

"We'll see."

"No, we won't. I'm serious, Hunter," she said.

He turned to face her on the bench and put his hand on the back of it. He ached. He wanted to pull her into his arms and kiss her until she stopped thinking and started reacting to him. Started to remember how good they were together, but he knew that he couldn't. He owed her the chance to process everything. He should back off, but it wasn't his way. He felt as if his team had been blitzed and he was scrambling to recover. He'd lost ground.

The end zone was farther away than before.

Wait. He thought the end zone had been Coach's files, and until this moment sitting on a park bench with Ferrin, he'd have sworn that was all he wanted. But he knew now he wanted her.

"But what about us?" he asked. He was tired of playing the long game. He wanted to get to the end zone and maybe retire with Ferrin by his side. But convincing her to give him a second chance was going to be hard.

"There is no us," she said.

"You can't ignore last night."

She stood up, put her hands on her hips and looked down at him. "I have to, Hunter. It's the only way I'm going to be able to function. It's just too confusing."

"Give me a chance," he said, getting to his feet next to her. "Let me prove to you that I am the man you thought I was."

She chewed her lower lip and he realized he'd never in his life wanted a do-over more than he did this one. He needed a second chance with her because even if he could fix the past for Stacia and her parents, he had no future without Ferrin.

"I really don't know."

"Just give me a chance. That's all I ask. Let's look through the boxes—"

"I haven't decided yet," she reminded him.

"Or not. Just don't shut me out."

She didn't answer him and he thought he'd lost all hope but then she nodded. "We can talk in a few days. I need a break."

"What kind of break?" he asked.

"I'm going home to Texas. I want to sit in my parents' house and let them spoil me."

Fair enough. She deserved that.

"When will you be back?"

"I have to look at flights but I'm thinking a week. I'll give you my answer then about the boxes or you can try your luck again with Coach. I'm done with men and football for now."

She walked away and all he could do was watch her go. He wasn't dumb and he knew when a woman was at her breaking point. Ferrin had been pushed too far today. He knew it was his fault. He wanted to make it up to her but she'd asked for time.

Maybe time would work in his favor. It couldn't hurt. And a gift. He'd send her something to show her that she meant more to him than access to some old files.

Thirteen

Ferrin's mom met her at the airport with a big hug and a sympathetic ear. She took her home, where Dean made himself scarce and they watched *Mean Girls* while eating Ben & Jerry's ice cream.

"So what happened?"

"I met a guy."

"How?"

"He's one of Dad's former players. He stopped by to see Coach," Ferrin said. She'd thought getting away from the pressure cooker of California would ease her pain but she was still hurt and confused. Maybe even more than before she'd left.

"A football player?"

"Yeah, Hunter Caruthers. He played in the NFL," she said.

"I think I've heard his name," her mom said, suddenly sounding evasive. "But I don't think it was because of football."

"It wasn't. He was arrested for murdering a college girl," Ferrin said. "He didn't do it."

"I figured that if he wasn't in jail," her mom said. "So what happened?"

Ferrin put her spoon in her bowl and set it on the coffee table, turning to face her mom. Suddenly she burst out crying and her mom reached over and pulled her into her arms.

"What happened, honey?"

"It got to the point where I didn't know what to believe. He didn't tell me everything he knew about what happened the night of the murder and then it came out on a TV program."

"Honey, I have a confession to make. Joy called me after she saw you on E! So I've heard about some of this. I just wanted to let you tell the story on your own terms and in your own time."

"It's okay, Mom. We were dating and he kept asking to see some of Dad's old stuff. Boxes the college sent over for him since they are retiring him. He said it was my decision, no pressure. But in the end, I couldn't take it. Was he using me? And why was I allowing that? I thought I was going crazy."

Her mom rubbed her back and stroked her hair, and Ferrin realized that despite being twenty-five, she needed that. "I don't know what to do."

Ferrin sat up, wiped her eyes and crossed her legs underneath her. She thought about Hunter. How he'd listened to her talk about her father and helped her learn how to catch. All the things they'd done together moved through her mind like a movie montage.

"You know, after Joy called me, I went on the E! News website and saw pictures of the two of you together," her mom said, "and I'll tell you something you might not want to hear. Ferrin, you looked happy. You looked like you were finally enjoying your life instead of just going about your routine. Maybe that's all he's meant to be to you. A memory of a wild time. Only you can decide that."

"Right now I'm hurt and a little angry."

"That will pass and then you'll be able to think about him more objectively. I have a couple of books I put on your nightstand for you to read," her mom said.

"Thanks."

"You're welcome. Dean is taking us shopping at the outlets tomorrow and then out to dinner. He said you deserve to be pampered."

Her stepdad was a great guy. Her mom had gotten lucky when she'd found him after the divorce. Ferrin realized that maybe she was afraid to trust Hunter because he was more like Coach than Dean. She knew that she'd never found any closure with Coach and she was beginning to think she never would.

She wasn't the child he'd wanted, but then she wasn't too sure what he did want.

It was easier to fall back into analyzing her relationship with her father than the mess between herself and Hunter. Hunter had disappointed her, she realized. She'd thought he was different. Not only from her father but also from all the other men she'd dated in the past. She'd wanted something from him that maybe he couldn't give her.

She just wasn't sure.

Gabi called her on the third day she was in Texas and Ferrin almost didn't answer the call. But at the last minute, she decided to pick up. They had a friendly conversation, and when Ferrin told Gabi that she was returning to California on Monday, they made plans for lunch.

Ferrin felt better after the call. She was beginning to look forward to going back to Carmel. To getting some closure. Once she got to her father's house, she'd take care of providing the material to the college for his tribute and then let Hunter and her father sort out if Hunter could look through those old boxes.

A part of her thought if there was any evidence in them that could shed light on the real murderer it needed to be found. But Ferrin knew she didn't have to be a part of that. She'd finish what she started in California and then come home and pretend that she'd never been there. Not the healthiest attitude but for right now that was all she had.

After one week in Texas, Ferrin wasn't sure she was ready to face Hunter or her father, but she was back in California. She arrived at San Francisco International Airport and made her way out toward baggage claim. When she got there, she noticed Hunter standing off to the side.

He was wearing faded blue jeans, a battered leather jacket, a baseball cap and sunglasses. He didn't say anything but she could tell from his body language the moment he spotted her.

She had thought she'd gotten over him. Or at least to a place where seeing him would be no biggie. She was wrong.

Her heartbeat raced and she felt something in her stomach that felt like excitement. She'd spent days reading about bad boys and the women who loved them. But it seemed she'd gleaned nothing from those books.

He lifted his hand from his side in a little wave and she waved back. She went to the baggage carousel to retrieve her suitcase and Hunter came to stand by her side.

"How was Texas?"

"Hot. Relaxing," she said. "Why are you here?"

"Because Gabi told me you were coming back today. After a long flight the last thing I want to deal with is a rental car and traffic. So I thought I'd offer my services as a driver."

A driver.

He hadn't texted or tried to call her the entire time she'd been gone. What had she expected? She'd told him to leave her be and he had. But she'd been disappointed. It had confirmed what she'd been telling herself—that he was simply using her and now that he was close to getting what he wanted, he didn't need her.

"Which bag is yours?" he asked.

She spotted the brightly colored floral-print bag that she used for travel. It was huge. Usually too heavy for her to carry.

She pointed to it and Hunter groaned as he lifted it off the carousel. "What do you have in this thing?"

"The essentials," she said. "You can put it down and I can get it."

"It's fine. So do you want a ride back to Carmel?" he asked.

"I…yes, I guess I would. We need to talk anyway," she said.

He nodded, shouldered her bag and led the way out of the airport to short-term parking. He'd brought his sports car with him and stowed her bag in the trunk before opening her door for her. "Top up or down?"

"Down," she said, hoping the breeze blowing around them as they drove would keep conversation to a minimum.

"Okay."

"I have been talking to Joy and your father about his stuff. And I think he's agreed to let me look through it, but only if you do it with me."

Her jaw dropped. "Why?"

"Your dad said that you thought it was important to take part in the tribute the college was doing."

She wrapped one arm around her waist and fumbled in her handbag for her sunglasses as they left the parking garage. The sky was clear and bright but there was a definite chill in the air coming off the bay.

"That's nice."

"Nice?"

"Yes. I reminded him that he had put football first all these years and it was time for him to at least be rewarded for that dedication. Do you still think you will find something in the files?"

"I hope so," he said. "Even if it's just a lead."

"I hope you find the answers you are looking for. What will you do then?" she asked.

"Pursue it."

She looked at him as he drove through the city traffic to the highway that would take them to the coast. He concentrated and drove with a singular skill. He noticed her watching and looked over at her for a split second before putting his eyes back on the road.

"What?"

"You didn't try to call," she said.

"You asked me not to. I wanted to give you time to relax and think. I'm here because I waited as long as I possibly could before seeing you again."

"A week."

"Yeah, I wanted to go to Texas after two days, but Kingsley said to respect the space you'd asked for."

"You talked to him about me?"

He nodded.

"I talked to Gabi about you."

"I want to start over, Ferrin. Me and you. But this time no secrets. No shame. No hidden agendas."

"I don't have anything I'm keeping from you," she said.

"Me either. You know everything now," he said. "Will you give me another chance?"

Saying no when what she wanted more than anything else was to say yes would be the dumbest thing in the world so she nodded.

Hunter pushed his sunglasses up on his head. "Is that a yes?"

"Yes."

"Oh, thank God. I thought… I thought I'd lost you forever," he said. He took her hand in his and squeezed it tight. "Thank you."

"This might not last. I have done a lot of thinking about us the last few days and I have come to the conclusion that you were like the bucket list. Something exciting and different. I'm just afraid to let myself think it might be more. It's different for you. You're used to playing games. I'm not."

But this had ceased being a game to Hunter that night they'd gone to Seconds and he'd realized that she meant more to him than he had expected. He was struck again by a paralyzing fear that he'd do the wrong thing and send her running away again.

"I'm not playing games with you, Ferrin. I had a lot of time to think and I realized that the longer I let this go on, the less chance I had of actually keeping you in my life."

"Letting what go on?"

"Manipulating you to get to Coach."

"Manipulating me?" she asked. "Are you kidding me?"

"No. Listen, I thought I'm used to doing whatever I have to in order to get what I want. You don't end up playing pro ball well if you aren't willing to sacrifice. And I have. But I can't do that any longer. I'd been trying to ensure you thought it was your idea to let me look at the boxes and then I realized that was no way to start a future."

"You think?" she asked.

"Dammit. I'm making a bigger mess of things, aren't I?" he asked.

"Well, you're certainly not making things better," she said. But he noticed she wasn't really mad.

"All I'm saying is that I'm sorry. I was wrong about a lot of things and I can make up reasons that are probably true, but what I know is that from the moment you opened that door and I realized that you were Coach's daughter everything changed."

She chewed on her lower lip and turned her head to the side to study him. "Why?"

He rubbed his hand over the back of his neck. The reasons were so deeply personal that he was afraid to say them out loud. "I guess I was attracted to you."

"Attracted?"

"Yes."

"Lust? That's the reason why things were different for you?" she asked.

He swallowed hard; he heard the tension in her voice and was pretty sure it was anger.

"No. But it's easier to say *desire* than *affection*. I don't believe in love at first sight."

"Me either. I mean, I get the science of attraction and I know about pheromones and hormones and how sometimes we see someone who our physiology makes us believe is the best one to mate with, but love at first sight…?"

"Yeah, crazy, right? But there it is, Ferrin. I think when I saw you, you knocked me on my ass. I figured I'd talk to Coach, get a yes about searching the boxes and then take you to dinner. But he said no and you said yes…everything got complicated then. I was still trying to get to the end zone, do what I'd come there to do, but you were slowly getting by my defenses without even trying."

She leaned closer to him and a waft of her floral perfume surrounded him. He closed his eyes, remembering the scent of it on the pillows in his bedroom. He wanted her. But he wanted her back for good. He was trying so hard to be cool and discuss this logically but there was no logic. He needed Ferrin to forgive him.

He knew that without her by his side he was never going to be able to figure out how to move on from the past. There were no answers that old videotapes could give him, that would bring him closure, if he alienated the one woman he needed to be with.

"Hunter, what are you trying to say?" she asked.

He took a deep breath, turning away from her and staring out at the highway. "I need you, Ferrin."

"Okay. How?"

"In my life. I thought I was saying that."

"Why now?" she asked. "The only way this will work is if we give each other time."

He nodded. He could do that. The end game. Ten yards at a time. But hell, he was tired of taking the ten-yards-at-a-time approach. He wanted a Hail Mary pass that he could catch and take into the end zone and end this game.

But he'd respect her wishes. He'd meant what he said about wanting to start over, and the only way he could do that would be to convince her she meant more to him than the past.

He wasn't sure how, but she'd taken control of his life. He knew she hadn't tried to do it. It had just happened. In those conversations about their fathers and football. The way they'd learned each other inside and out by spending time together.

He pulled to a stop in front of her house, parked the car and turned to face her.

"Will you let me come in with you?" he asked. "I want to talk to you about a few things I've uncovered in your father's office."

She sighed and looked over at him. "Yes. When did you find the time to go through my dad's things?"

"I'll tell you when we are inside. I think this will surprise you," he said.

He got out of the car and took a deep breath. The key was to be cool and act normal. That was all he had to do.

Ten yards at a time. It felt like the longest game of his life and each ten yards he ran for was longer than the ten yards before. He was tired and ready for it to be over, but then he remembered something his father had said to him a long time ago. There are no shortcuts in life.

And he had only himself to blame for trying to take one with Ferrin.

Fourteen

Ferrin didn't want to talk about the past or football. She was still trying to figure out exactly what it was Hunter had been trying to communicate in the car. He'd sounded as if he cared for her. Okay, maybe even loved her but wasn't sure enough of himself or maybe of her to say it.

She'd had a long talk with her mom about him while she'd been in Texas. And that was part of the reason why it was so easy for her to remain calm now. Her mom had pointed out that Hunter was the first man she'd been in a relationship with that she was actually upset about when it ended. Her mom had pointed out that Ferrin had never allowed herself to really get emotionally involved before.

She walked up the path to the house; Hunter was behind her carrying her bag. The door opened and a large man came bounding down the steps. He was holding something in his left hand and as he got closer Ferrin noticed that his nose was bleeding and that she recognized him.

"Graham? What are you doing here?"

He seemed surprised to see her. "Ferrin, I thought you were still in Texas. I stopped by to get a videotape for the tribute we are putting together about your dad."

Graham's face was flushed and his salt-and-pepper hair was disheveled. She put her hand out to steady him as he looked past her and sort of feinted to the left. "You have a nosebleed. I have a tissue in my purse. Why don't you sit down on the front porch and I will get you some ice for it."

He wiped his hand under his nose and looked down at the smear of blood on the back of his hand as Hunter joined her.

"Coach Peters, nice to see you," Hunter said, holding out his hand.

"Hunter. I'm surprised you're back in California," Graham said. "I'd avoid it if I had your reputation."

Ferrin stepped in front of Hunter. "Excuse me? I think you know as well as everyone at the college that Hunter was falsely accused."

Hunter put his hand on her shoulder and shifted her to the side. "It's okay, Ferrin."

"Stop him!" Joy yelled from the door. "He's stolen that tape."

Ferrin's gaze met Graham's and he shoved her hard to the ground as he tried to sprint around Hunter. Hunter took a running leap and tackled Graham to the ground. Graham tried to wriggle out of Hunter's grip but Hunter went for the tape, not the man, and wrested it from Graham's hands.

They heard the sound of sirens just as Hunter stood up. Ferrin got to her feet, rubbing her side, as Hunter stood over Graham until the cops arrived.

Joy came down to meet them.

"I called 911," she greeted the cops. "He hit the coach and stole some of his property."

"It's the property of the college," Graham said. "Everyone in this house is crazy. The housekeeper. The old man who punched me and this guy who tackled me. I'm thinking of pressing charges."

"Let's get everyone's statements first. I'm Officer Daniels and this is Officer Stevens," the first cop said. He took Graham's arm in his. "Are you okay? Do you need medical assistance?"

"I'm fine."

"Can I go check on my dad?" Ferrin asked.

"Yes," Officer Stevens said. "I'll come with you."

Hunter caught her hand in his. "Are you okay?"

She nodded. "Are you?"

"Yes."

Ferrin went into the house with Officer Stevens on her heels. She found her father in his desk chair in his study. His lip was bleeding and his shirt was torn.

"Dad! Are you okay?"

"Yes," he said. "Just feeling stupid."

"What happened?" Officer Stevens asked.

"Graham Peters broke into my house and tried to

steal my property," Coach said. "I think he's responsible for Stacia Krushnik's death."

"Really?" Ferrin asked.

"Yes. There was something odd about that time, and when Hunter stopped by a few days ago to talk about what was going on in the gym, I remembered the tapes we had. I thought I'd review them before Hunter did and I saw…well, I saw that poor girl being raped and killed by Graham. I called him to tell him I knew what he'd done and that it was time to turn himself in."

"Dad, that was—"

"Stupid, I know. Did you get the tape?" he asked. "It's on the tape."

"We got it," Ferrin said. "Can you arrest him, Officer Stevens?"

"We can hold him but the DA will have to review the tape before we see if charges can be brought against him," Officer Stevens said. "We can arrest him for breaking into your house and assaulting your father."

Ferrin went to her dad's side as the officer asked him a few more questions. She dug around in her purse for a tissue and reached over to dab at the blood on his lip but he stopped her. He squeezed her hand and then held it while he continued talking to the police.

Graham was taken to the station. A copy of the tape and the rest of Coach's files were requested by the district attorney's office. It was almost midnight before her father was safely tucked into his bed and Ferrin had a moment to think. Hunter and Kingsley had both given new statements to the district attorney.

Ferrin didn't know when she'd see Hunter again.

Joy had gone home and Ferrin had given her the next few days off.

She had showered and changed into a pair of yoga pants and a long-sleeved shirt but couldn't sleep. She went back downstairs to the kitchen and made herself a cup of tea. She kept looking at her phone and realized that she was waiting for Hunter. They hadn't had a chance to talk and she was worried about him.

Hunter left the district attorney's office at a little after midnight and drove to Ferrin's house. He knew it was late and he should go home but he needed to see her. To think that tape had been in a box the past ten years and he and Kingsley had walked around with the guilt and the condemnation while Graham Peters had hidden in plain sight.

He'd taken time to call Stacia's parents and talk to them. They had believed him when he'd been released, but then they'd seen the same evidence that Hunter had. The proof that another man was responsible but there was no DNA evidence to link it to any of the players. That was the rub. They'd tested all the men in the frat house and every football player, looking for a DNA match, but had never tested the coaches. In hindsight everyone was saying that was something that shouldn't have been overlooked. But at the time the DA had been determined to get the case out of the spotlight once the charges against Hunter and Kingsley had been dropped.

There was still so much to do but Hunter needed to find Ferrin first. Today had made him realize all the hemming and hawing he'd done in the car was ridiculous. He loved her. He needed to tell her and convince her to really give him a second chance. And though he'd said he'd had no more secrets he knew he'd hidden his love for her and he didn't want to do that. Not anymore.

Knowing what happened to Stacia had set him free and he knew that he'd been waiting for that before he felt safe loving Ferrin. And asking Ferrin to take a chance on loving him. He hadn't been able to before but he could now.

He texted her because it was after midnight and he didn't want to knock on her door and freak her out. Or have her send him away. He needed her. He hadn't realized how much until Gabi had shown up at the DA's office and Hunter had watched her and Kingsley leave together.

Hey. Are you still awake? Can I come over?

Yes. I'm waiting for you.

Waiting for him?

He liked the sound of that.

He got out of the car. The air was crisp and cool. The sky was full of stars and the moon was big and bright, lighting his way toward Ferrin's house. As he walked up the steps he remembered Graham shoving Ferrin. His knuckles ached from the punch he'd gotten in but he didn't regret it. He wished he'd punched Graham more than once.

The door opened and Ferrin stood in the doorway. Backlit from the hallway, her thick black hair curled around her shoulders as she leaned against the door-jamb. He hurried up the steps and scooped her up in his arms, kicking the door closed behind him. He knew they needed to talk but he needed her first.

It was primitive and primal but none of that mattered. He buried his hands in her hair as he plundered her mouth. Her hands were on his back, holding him tightly to her. He pulled her off her feet as he leaned back against the wall. She tasted of mint and tea and he realized how hungry he'd been for her.

He'd been parched for this woman and not just since she'd gone to Texas. He'd been missing her in his life for too long. He pulled his mouth free but he couldn't lift his head. He rubbed his lips against hers and she wrapped her thighs around his hips.

He settled his hands on her butt and carried her down the hall to the kitchen, where the lights were on. He set her on the counter on the island and stood between her legs. She probably wanted to talk.

He should let her talk. But he could see the shape of her nipples beneath her light-colored shirt and he lifted his hand to trace one, and then he had to kiss her again.

He braced one hand next to her hips on the counter and leaned over her, taking her mouth with his again. His tongue thrust deep into her and she held his head, rubbing her fingers against his scalp in a way that made everything in him tingle. His heartbeat was so loud he was sure she could hear it echoing around the kitchen.

She sucked his lower lip into her mouth and bit it, causing him to lift his head and look down at her. When he put his hands on her waist and drew her closer to him. She pulled back and bit his lip again.

"What was that for?"

"Making me think you might not come back tonight," she said.

"Were you waiting for me?"

"Duh," she said. She framed his face with her hands and stared into his eyes, and he felt something that had been tightly held inside him for so long break free. He dropped his head, resting it against her torso and hugging her closer. He wasn't letting go.

She clung to him just as fiercely, her fingers stroking the back of his head and his neck until he lifted his head again.

"I love you, Ferrin. I hedged it earlier in the car but that's the truth. I can't imagine a future for myself without you."

She leaned down and kissed his jaw, ran her fingers over his beard as she nibbled her way to his ear.

"I love you, too," she whispered into his ear. "I'm afraid."

"Me, too," he admitted. "I've never cared for anyone like this before."

"Me either."

He pushed his hands up under her shirt and caressed her back. Somehow knowing they were in the same boat made it easier to deal with his emotions. He wasn't alone. In fact it felt as if he had the kind of partner he'd been unconsciously searching for in his life for a long time.

"What are we going to do next?" she asked.

"I'm going to make love to you until we both fall into an exhausted sleep and tomorrow we'll figure everything else out."

"I like the sound of that," she said.

He took the hem of her shirt in both hands and drew it up and over her head, tossing it aside. She put her hands behind her on the counter and leaned back, thrusting her breasts up and into prominence.

He lowered his head between them, plumping them up on each side of his face, and rubbed his beard over the tips before sucking one of her nipples into his mouth. She held his head to her breast and arched underneath him.

Her legs parted and she shifted forward on the counter so that he was pressed more tightly to her. He wrapped one arm around her hips and pulled her yoga pants down. He wanted to take things slow but he felt a sense of urgency. Desire and lust had combined with his newly realized feelings of love and he had to have her. Had to make her his so that she knew that he was never going to let her go again.

He stepped back to take off his jeans and watched as Ferrin shimmied out of her yoga pants and her panties.

Hunter had never seen anything more beautiful than Ferrin. Her skin was creamy and pale, her nipples pink and the hair between her legs dark and neatly trimmed. He'd seen many different sides of her but he realized for the first time he was seeing all of her. Maybe it was that she felt comfortable now that she knew he loved her, but he'd never in his life seen any woman who could hold a candle to her in this moment.

"You're gorgeous," he said, his voice deep and raspy. He knew he was lucky to be able to speak since every instinct he had was screaming for him to climb on top of her and thrust himself deep inside her body until he came.

But he wanted this to last. At least for a little bit longer. He'd never said those words to a woman and he wanted to show her how much she meant to him.

It was hard to believe that he was finally free of the past and that he had the woman he wanted here with him now. She was naked and spread out on the counter waiting for him.

She lifted one hand and crooked her finger at him and he took a step toward her. He ran his hands slowly over her torso, almost afraid to believe that after everything they'd been through together she was his now. He felt as though he'd run his last ten yards and they were in the end zone now.

Reaching out, she took his erection in her hand. She shifted forward and stroked him up and down, cupping him with her other hand. She smoothed her finger over the tip and then continued to caress his length.

She kissed his neck and then made a little moan of disappointment. "Take your shirt off."

He moved so quickly he almost tore the fabric, wrenching his shirt up and over his head and tossing it aside. She nibbled at his chest, slowly following the line of hair that went down his stomach. She let go of his hard-on and put her arms around him, cupping his buttocks and drawing him closer to her. She spread her thighs and wrapped her legs around his hips. She shifted until the tip of his erection was poised at her entrance.

He pushed into her slowly and then stopped. He caught her chin in his hand and tipped her head back. Their eyes met as he slowly pushed his way into her body, not stopping this time until he was fully seated.

She changed position slightly and he slid a tiny bit deeper. He looked into her eyes and saw the future that he wanted. Saw the woman who would be his partner in and out of bed.

She clenched herself around him and then lowered her head to nip at his nipple. He drew his hips back and thrust into her. Tangling his hands in her hair, he took her long and hard, driving into her again and again until he felt a shiver down his spine and he knew he was close to his climax.

She dug her nails into his back and drew them downward, lightly abrading his skin and making his hips jerk forward. He was holding on by the tiniest thread of control.

Her hands came back up to the back of his head as she rocked her hips against his. Her nipples rubbed against his chest and he groaned. He looked up at her and saw her head tossing side to side as she rode him.

He leaned down and caught one of her nipples in his teeth, scraping very gently. Her hips moved faster, demanding more, but he kept the pace slow, steady, wanting her to come again before he did.

He suckled her nipple and rotated his hips to catch her pleasure point with each thrust. Then he felt her hands clenching his hair as she threw her head back.

He reached between their bodies and found her center, rubbing it with his finger until she arched in his arms, calling his name.

He didn't want to come yet. Didn't want this first time when they'd both admitted they loved each other to end so fast. He pulled out of her and pulled her down, letting her slide against his body until her feet touched the floor.

"Did you?" she asked. She sounded dazed. Her lips were swollen and wet from his kisses.

"Not yet," he said. "We only get to make love knowing we both love each other for the first time once."

Her skin was flushed with arousal; her nipples still hard. She ran her hands up and down his body. "Okay, but I want to you to come."

"I'm going to," he said. He turned her in his arms and bent her forward over the counter. She looked back over her shoulder at him as he kissed the nape of her neck. He had one hand on her stomach, his fingers moving lower. He rubbed his hand over her mound and then parted her until he could touch her clit. He bit her neck and shifted so that he could thrust one leg between hers, forcing her legs apart.

He kissed his way down her back, slowly moving between her shoulders blades and then lower to the tiny dimple that was just above the curve of her ass. He bit at the small of her back, felt the answering shiver in her body as he straightened back up.

He used his other hand to draw her hips back and then leaned into the curve of her buttocks, rubbing his erection against her. He shifted his hips, found her feminine center and then thrust into her. She moaned and arched against him. He went deeper than he had before and continued to rub her clit as he thrust into her. He braced his hand on the counter in front of her and she leaned down and sucked his thumb into her mouth as she continued thrusting her hips back against him.

He felt so tight and hard, and shivers of desire were shaking his body, but he was determined to make this last. But only moments later, she arched in his arms and came again, this time calling out his name.

He started to thrust harder and deeper. He twisted his hand on her hair and drew her head back, leaning over her, which drove him deeper into her body as he found her mouth. She sucked on his tongue and he shuddered, drawing back his hips as he thrust into her one last time, reaching his own climax. He continued to thrust until he was completely empty. She shuddered and wrapped her arms around him, letting her head fall to his chest. He held her close as the sweat dried on their bodies.

They stayed there holding each other, his hands running up and down her back. She sighed. "I didn't think I'd ever fall for a football player."

"I didn't think I'd ever find you," Hunter admitted. His mom had despaired that he'd ever get over Stacia and find a woman. She had five sons and no daughters-in-law, no grandkids, and it bothered her. He hadn't really thought about marriage; given the fact that his life was tied to the tragedy of Stacia's death it hadn't been an option. But he knew it was now. He wanted Ferrin to be his wife. He had a feeling she might say it was too soon so he'd wait a little while until he could show her the kind of man he really was.

He'd woo her and seduce her and leave her in no doubt of how much he loved her and was committed to her.

He hugged her closer to him. His hands tangled in her hair, the scent of woman and sex filling each breath he took. He could have stayed like that all night but he wanted to make love to her again. He stooped to pick up their discarded clothes, handing them to her before he lifted her in his arms and carried her up the stairs.

"I can't believe how strong you are. You really impressed me when you tackled Graham today."

"Thank you," he said. "Now I know why I've been working out all these years."

"To tackle people?" she asked, wrapping her around his shoulders.

"No, to carry you. I like you in my arms."

"I like it, too," she said.

"Which room is yours?" he asked quietly.

She pointed to it and he carried her inside her room, setting her on her feet next to her bed.

"Want to have that bath we never got to take together?" she asked.

He nodded, realizing that there were so many things that he wanted to do with her and he could take his time with them because they had forever.

She went into the bathroom and he followed her. She was bent over the side of the tub checking the taps and mixing the water and he stood in the doorway watching her.

He wondered if he'd ever get used to this. To having her in his life and the feelings of lust and love flowing through him. He hoped he never did. He never wanted this to be routine. He wanted to always look at her and see the woman who had saved him without even knowing she was doing it.

"You okay?" she asked, glancing back at him.

"More than okay," he admitted.

Epilogue

Hunter's mom was in heaven. Actually, Ferrin's mom was pretty pleased, as well. Hunter had asked her to marry him on Valentine's Day on the top of the Empire State Building. It had been pretty funny when he'd forgotten about the metal detectors that everyone had to go through and security had stopped them.

He'd had his baseball cap and sunglasses on and took them off to talk to the officers. They weren't Bills fans and gave him a hard time for a few of the touchdowns he'd made in his playing days against the Jets. But Hunter had taken it in stride, ultimately going down on one knee and asking Ferrin to marry him in front of the security guards.

She'd of course said yes and they'd taken pictures at

the top of the Empire State Building. Both decided to keep their security office proposal a secret.

Now it was the end of June and she was getting married.

"You look so beautiful," her mom said as she adjusted one of the curls around her face.

"She does," Gabi agreed. Gabi was serving as her matron of honor, having married Kingsley in a Christmas wedding. Zara was serving as flower girl and Conner as the ring bearer. They'd posed for photos earlier and Ferrin had taken a moment to count her blessings.

She and her father were slowly getting closer. One of the things that Hunter had wanted to show her was that he'd found a collection of newspaper and magazine clippings that she'd written and her father had kept over the years. She and Hunter had spent a few days in Carmel at the end of May and Coach was coming to the wedding today. Since it would be awkward for Dean and Coach if one or the other gave her away, Ferrin had decided to walk herself down the aisle.

Hunter had four brothers and had avoided having a huge wedding party by telling them he was having Kingsley as his best man and that was it. Kingsley and Hunter had a bond that Hunter didn't have with his brothers.

Hunter was getting more and more comfortable with his past. Graham had confessed and taken a plea deal to avoid a trial, and that had brought closure to Hunter and Kingsley and to Stacia's parents, who had been plagued by unanswered questions.

"Ready to do this?" her mom asked.

"Is it time?" Ferrin countered.

"I think so. I see Hunter—he's so good-looking."

She thought so, too. But more than that he was a good man. He'd spent the past year proving it to her every day. He still liked to keep things to himself and to try to shield her from things he thought would upset her. But he was coming to know she could handle herself.

Hunter had applied for a job coaching football at the college she worked at and in the fall term he'd start as the special teams coach. He was looking forward to it. And so was Ferrin. It had been hard the past year while she taught and he continued to travel with his charity. But they'd made it work. They were both looking forward to spending more time together.

She heard the beginning of the Wedding Canon and Zara squealed with joy. "It's almost my turn."

Ferrin went over to the little girl and put her hand on her shoulder. "Thank you for helping make my wedding day so special."

"You're welcome. I love my dress. My sisters didn't get one this fancy," Zara said.

Ferrin and Gabi both laughed. Conner was carefully watching the wedding planner at the end of the aisle, waiting for his signal. He was dressed in a tux with tails and looked adorable.

Everyone in the wedding party slowly trickled out of the room and Ferrin took a deep breath as she got ready to step out into the church. There was no room for doubts in her mind as she spotted Hunter at the front of the church waiting for her.

Her breath caught in her throat and her heart was

filled with so much love. She felt so happy and lucky to have found this man to share her life with.

As soon as she was by his side, he took her hand in his. The ceremony flew by in a blur and it wasn't long before he was kissing her.

There was a loud whoop from one of Hunter's brothers, which made Hunter laugh.

The reception went by almost as fast as the vows and before he knew it, they were alone in the honeymoon suite. "Mrs. Caruthers, you've made me the happiest man in the world."

"Me, too!"

He tumbled her on the bed and they made love. Sleep eluded them afterward and they talked about their dreams for the future and their life together.

Hunter had a lot of plans, and he talked about them constantly. He held her close as if he were still not quite sure that she was his. And she held him back. This football player, the last man in the world she'd ever have expected to fall for. The man she loved with her body and soul.

* * * * *

If you liked this novel, pick up all the books in the
SONS OF PRIVILEGE *series by*
USA TODAY *bestselling author Katherine Garbera*

THE GREEK TYCOON'S SECRET HEIR
THE WEALTHY FRENCHMAN'S PROPOSITION
THE SPANISH ARISTOCRAT'S WOMAN
HIS BABY AGENDA
HIS SEDUCTION GAME PLAN

All available now, only from Harlequin Desire!

***

*If you're on Twitter, tell us what you think
of Harlequin Desire! #harlequindesire*

HD15

REQUEST YOUR FREE BOOKS!

◆ HARLEQUIN

Presents®

2 FREE NOVELS PLUS
2 FREE GIFTS!

PASSION GUARANTEED SEDUCTION

YES! Please send me 2 FREE Harlequin Presents® novels and my 2 FREE gifts (gifts are worth about $10). After receiving them, if I don't wish to receive any more books, I can return the shipping statement marked "cancel." If I don't cancel, I will receive 6 brand-new novels every month and be billed just $4.30 per book in the U.S. or $5.24 per book in Canada. That's a saving of at least 13% off the cover price! It's quite a bargain! Shipping and handling is just 50¢ per book in the U.S. and 75¢ per book in Canada.* I understand that accepting the 2 free books and gifts places me under no obligation to buy anything. I can always return a shipment and cancel at any time. Even if I never buy another book, the two free books and gifts are mine to keep forever.

106/306 HDN GHRP

Name _____ (PLEASE PRINT)

Address _____ Apt. #

City _____ State/Prov. _____ Zip/Postal Code

Signature (if under 18, a parent or guardian must sign)

Mail to the **Reader Service:**
IN U.S.A.: P.O. Box 1867, Buffalo, NY 14240-1867
IN CANADA: P.O. Box 609, Fort Erie, Ontario L2A 5X3

**Are you a current subscriber to Harlequin Presents® books
and want to receive the larger-print edition?
Call 1-800-873-8635 or visit www.ReaderService.com.**

* Terms and prices subject to change without notice. Prices do not include applicable taxes. Sales tax applicable in N.Y. Canadian residents will be charged applicable taxes. Offer not valid in Quebec. This offer is limited to one order per household. Not valid for current subscribers to Harlequin Presents books. All orders subject to credit approval. Credit or debit balances in a customer's account(s) may be offset by any other outstanding balance owed by or to the customer. Please allow 4 to 6 weeks for delivery. Offer available while quantities last.

Your Privacy—The Reader Service is committed to protecting your privacy. Our Privacy Policy is available online at www.ReaderService.com or upon request from the Reader Service.

We make a portion of our mailing list available to reputable third parties that offer products we believe may interest you. If you prefer that we not exchange your name with third parties, or if you wish to clarify or modify your communication preferences, please visit us at www.ReaderService.com/consumerschoice or write to us at Reader Service Preference Service, P.O. Box 9062, Buffalo, NY 14240-9062. Include your complete name and address.

HPI5

REQUEST YOUR FREE BOOKS!

2 FREE NOVELS
FROM THE ROMANCE COLLECTION
PLUS 2 FREE GIFTS!

YES! Please send me 2 FREE novels from the Romance Collection and my 2 FREE gifts (gifts are worth about $10). After receiving them, if I don't wish to receive any more books, I can return the shipping statement marked "cancel." If I don't cancel, I will receive 4 brand-new novels every month and be billed just $6.49 per book in the U.S. or $6.99 per book in Canada. That's a savings of at least 19% off the cover price. It's quite a bargain! Shipping and handling is just 50¢ per book in the U.S. and 75¢ per book in Canada.* I understand that accepting the 2 free books and gifts places me under no obligation to buy anything. I can always return a shipment and cancel at any time. Even if I never buy another book, the two free books and gifts are mine to keep forever.

194/394 MDN GH4D

Name   (PLEASE PRINT)

Address   Apt. #

City   State/Prov.   Zip/Postal Code

Signature (if under 18, a parent or guardian must sign)

Mail to the **Reader Service:**
IN U.S.A.: P.O. Box 1867, Buffalo, NY 14240-1867
IN CANADA: P.O. Box 609, Fort Erie, Ontario L2A 5X3

Want to try two free books from another line?
Call 1-800-873-8635 or visit www.ReaderService.com.

* Terms and prices subject to change without notice. Prices do not include applicable taxes. Sales tax applicable in N.Y. Canadian residents will be charged applicable taxes. Offer not valid in Quebec. This offer is limited to one order per household. Not valid for current subscribers to the Romance Collection or the Romance/Suspense Collection. All orders subject to credit approval. Credit or debit balances in a customer's account(s) may be offset by any other outstanding balance owed by or to the customer. Please allow 4 to 6 weeks for delivery. Offer available while quantities last.

Your Privacy—The Reader Service is committed to protecting your privacy. Our Privacy Policy is available online at www.ReaderService.com or upon request from the Reader Service.

We make a portion of our mailing list available to reputable third parties that offer products we believe may interest you. If you prefer that we not exchange your name with third parties, or if you wish to clarify or modify your communication preferences, please visit us at www.ReaderService.com/consumerchoice or write to us at Reader Service Preference Service, P.O. Box 9062, Buffalo, NY 14240-9062. Include your complete name and address.

ROM15

READERSERVICE.COM

Manage your account online!

- Review your order history
- Manage your payments
- Update your address

> **We've designed the Reader Service website just for you.**

Enjoy all the features!

- Discover new series available to you, and read excerpts from any series.
- Respond to mailings and special monthly offers.
- Connect with favorite authors at the blog.
- Browse the Bonus Bucks catalog and online-only exculsives.
- Share your feedback.

Visit us at:

ReaderService.com